Guarding the Bootlegger's Widow

Denise Devine

USA Today Bestselling Author

A Sweet Historical Roaring Twenties Novel

Moonshine Madness Series – Book 2

Wild Prairie Rose Books

Guarding the Bootlegger's Widow

(Moonshine Madness Series - Book 2)

Print Edition

Copyright 2020 by Denise Devine

https://www.deniseannettedevine.com

ISBN: 978-1-943124-18-3

Published in the United States of America

Wild Prairie Rose Books

Edited by L. Nies, D. Pearson, J. Dalton

Cover Design by Raine English

Also available as an audiobook.

Want to stay in touch with me? Sign up for my newsletter at **https://eepurl.com/csOJZL** and receive a *free novella*. You'll be the first to know about my new releases, sales, and special events.

For Ken

Love ya…

Prologue

St. Paul, Minnesota - 1926

According to the gossip on the streets of St. Paul, my late husband was a man of many secrets. One of the most widely spread stories I found intriguing, but also amusing, involved a secluded hideout where he supposedly had a wall literally lined with stacks of cash. If he did, Gus had taken this information to the grave because he'd never shared it with me.

Gus had been a bootlegger who'd made his fortune running "Minnesota 13," the Dom Perignon of bootlegged whiskey from two Minnesota counties—Stearns and Morrison—to distributors in the Dakotas and Chicago. Ruthless and powerful, "Lucky" Gus LeDoux had earned an unfathomable amount of money and gained a notorious reputation, but made permanent enemies along the way. I always knew someday he'd die a violent death. I just never envisioned it would be by *my* hand.

I hadn't planned to shoot my husband; I'd acted purely in self-defense. It did no good to dwell on it, but the memory of that horrific, life-altering day still haunted me…

Desperate to escape his life of crime, I'd run away from my husband and found refuge working as a domestic servant in the home of a private investigator. Gus eventually found out and stormed my place of employment, forcing me to leave with him. As Federal agents surrounded the area, two agents tried to apprehend him and he gunned them down—while I helplessly watched. My husband was known for his brutality, but to witness it firsthand horrified me and caused me to fear not only for my safety but also for the wellbeing of my unborn child. I refused to go on and told Gus I wanted nothing more to do with him. He roared that if he couldn't have me, no one would, and he tried to choke me.

Determined to protect my baby, I grabbed the gun from his shoulder holster. We struggled. The gun went off. The memory of that deadly, piercing sound still left me numb; a stark reminder that my son, now three and a half months old, would never know his father. And I was to blame.

Only one other person saw what happened, but I knew Will Van Elsberg would never divulge my secret to anyone. To rescue me from the fray, he had lifted me in his arms and carried me to a secure place to keep me safe, proving himself to be the only true hero I'd ever known.

The events of that dark, rainy afternoon altered my life forever. As Gus' widow, I inherited a fortune and became the sole parent of my newborn son. Though I was on my own for the first time in my life, I felt safe. I was free.

Then fate pulled me back to the dark side of Gus' world, the most dangerous place I could be.

Chapter One

Mid-March, 1926

The silky fabric of my evening dress shimmered; Cartier diamonds sparkled on my neck and ears. My hair had been meticulously styled in soft, marcel waves and spit curls. I freshened my skin with a spritz of Parisian perfume, humming a tune as I waited for my escorts to arrive.

The Katzenbaum brothers were taking me out to dinner. Harv and Marv were my late husband's attorney and accountant, respectively, but with Gus' passing late last summer, they'd become like fathers to me. They were stern taskmasters, expecting me to learn every detail of how to successfully manage Gus' legitimate businesses. At the same time, however, they were fiercely protective of me and truly cared about my happiness. They insisted I needed a night out on the town to bolster my morale, but I suspected they'd decided it was high time the world got a glimpse of Gus LeDoux's rich, young widow. The woman who had taken the reins of his investments.

The shiny black Rolls Royce Phantom arrived at Mamma's house at seven o'clock that evening. The epitome of elegance and wealth, the long, shiny vehicle looked strangely out of place in Mamma's modest neighborhood on the east side of St. Paul. An armored touring car carrying a cadre of bodyguards with Tommy guns sat close behind it.

"They're here!" my fourteen-year-old sister, Francie, exclaimed, waving to Harv and Marv Katzenbaum from the living room window.

Her long flaxen braids fell to her waist as she whirled around and stared at me longingly through wide blue eyes. "I wish I could go with you, Char. I want to wear a pretty dress and shawl like yours!"

I wished I could take her with me to give her a much-needed respite from our family issues, but minors weren't allowed where I was going. Mrs. Olson, our neighbor, usually took care of Mamma and my son, Julien, when I had to leave the house on errands. Unfortunately, she had a cold today, so Francie had agreed to take her place and earn the dollar I would have paid to Mrs. Olson.

I retouched my lips with Max Factor lipstick from a new tube I'd just purchased in cherry red matte—my favorite color. Then I went into Mamma's bedroom, a small, corner room on the main floor to say goodbye. She lay in her bed, pale and tired, listening to the radio. Mamma had been ill with a bad heart for as long as I could remember. In high school, I'd struggled to support her by working as a housekeeper at Finnegan's Hotel. Once I married Gus, we wanted to take her into our home, but she begged us to stay in her own place and hang onto what little independence she had. After Gus died, I closed up our mansion on Summit Avenue and moved back into Mamma's little house. Until Mamma left this world my place was to stay with her and take care of her. She and Francie were the only family little Julien and I had.

Well, except for my alcoholic father, but Papa only came around when he couldn't get a free meal anywhere else. He'd stay for one night, then he'd be gone again, often for months.

I took Mamma's hand. "I'm leaving now, but I won't stay out late."

She slowly opened her eyes. "You have a nice time, Charlotte," she whispered, "and don't worry about the baby. Francie will take good care of him."

I didn't worry as much about my son as I was concerned for *her*. She looked so frail—so exhausted. I gently patted her hand. "I'll bring home some cheesecake for you and Francie." Sadly, Mamma's appetite had become so small she probably wouldn't eat more than a bite, but if it made her day a little brighter, that's all that mattered.

The brothers were taking me to a new dining establishment called the Tansy Club and I had been looking forward to it for a week. I'd only had one social outing since I'd given birth to Julien last November and that was to treat Francie to a movie. I grabbed my knee-length sable coat from the closet and my beaded handbag from the kitchen table just as the chauffeur knocked on the front door. With a hug, I told my sister goodbye, slipped into my coat, and hurried out into the waning light of a chilly March evening.

The chauffeur escorted me to the car and opened the rear passenger door. Harv slid out to allow me to get in and greeted me with his customary kiss on the cheek. I climbed inside the vehicle's gray velvet interior and sat next to Marv. "Good evening!" I said cheerily.

"Good evening, my dear," Marv replied in his gravelly voice. The wrinkles in his wizened face deepened when he smiled.

Both men were gray-haired and in their sixties, but Marv, the accountant, was the younger one by a year or two and had never married. He had arthritis and high blood pressure but he refused to quit drinking or smoking his Camel cigarettes.

Harv was an attorney who'd lost his wife and only child years ago in childbirth. He wore rimless spectacles and carried a gold pocket watch on a chain nestled in the pocket of his vest.

Harv and Marv, known as "the brothers" were extremely intelligent and shrewd when it came to making money. Two of the most powerful businessmen in St. Paul.

Harv settled in on my right as the car door shut. Within a few moments, we were on our way to a speakeasy for dinner. I looked forward to an exciting evening.

*　　*　　*

The Tansy Club was situated along the shore of White Bear Lake, north of St. Paul. The Rolls Royce pulled up to the back of a large, old barn and dropped us off at the door. The exterior, weathered and plain, didn't look like anything special, but the moment Harv recited the passcode, the security guard opened the door and allowed us into an extraordinary world only available to those who were invited.

After Harv checked our coats and hats, a man with brown hair parted down the center, and wearing a black suit ushered us through a doorway hung with two sets of red and gold damask brocade portieres—door curtains—one set on each side. The interior of the lively speakeasy had walls paneled in fumed oak, hanging lights with shades made of art nouveau glass, and a ceiling covered in gold leaf. A stage in the far corner of the room hosted a small orchestra. The lead singer, a tall, curvaceous redhead in a sparkling burgundy gown crooned Fanny Brice's trademark song, "My Man" to a happy crowd on the dance floor.

The Tansy Club was certainly one of the nicest speakeasies I'd ever been to, but it couldn't compare with the glamorous nightclub that Gus and I had once owned. Before the Feds shut it down, La Coquette had been *the* place to be seen in St. Paul. Now the building was just a dark, empty shell set back in the trees near the corner of Snelling and West Seventh Street.

At our table, the host pulled out my chair. I sat gracefully and allowed him to drop my linen napkin on my lap. "The food here smells wonderful," I murmured as my nostrils filled with the mouth-watering aroma of steak. My stomach growled with hunger.

"Here is your wine list, sir," the host said, handing a leather-bound folder to Harv. He nodded to the man and began to leisurely peruse the selection, indicating he wasn't in any hurry to dine. He ordered a bottle of Bordeaux, which must have cost him a pretty penny considering prohibition currently dictated the law of the land.

Our waiter returned with the bottle, opened it, and offered Harv the cork. He examined it, sniffed it then handed it back with a nod of approval. The waiter poured a small amount into a stemmed wineglass for his inspection. Harv swirled the wine lightly, held the glass to his nose then took a sip. Another nod indicated his pleasure with his selection.

I sat with my hands in my lap, observing the ritual as an odd sensation swept over my body. I could feel the intense gaze of someone watching me. Puzzled, I glanced around, and as I scanned the crowded room goosebumps spread the length of my arms. Everywhere I looked, people were staring—at me. Some were discreet, whispering amongst themselves. Others openly assessed me. Had my ten-month retreat from society caused such a stir that my appearance tonight had shocked everyone? Or did it stem from the fact that my late husband's reputation made people overly cautious of me? Most people probably didn't know that I had always been in Gus' shadow. Finding myself the center of attention made me feel like a bug in a glass jar. I pulled my shawl tighter about my shoulders and tried to ignore the curious looks directed my way, forcing myself to concentrate on the conversation around the table instead.

"In a couple of weeks, I'm goin' to visit a lady friend," Marv carried on in his raspy tone. "Takin' the Oriental Limited out to Seattle for a month." He spent the next ten minutes telling me how he'd met her at a wedding in St. Paul and how much he was looking forward to seeing her again.

Harv, a soft-spoken man of few words, preferred to relax and sip his wine as Marv and I talked. Though he rarely showed it, I knew Harv was taking in more than our conversation. He had a way of appearing at ease while maintaining an acute awareness of his surroundings.

A handsome man in a tuxedo approached our table. The brothers received him cordially, but I could see the slight bulge of a shoulder holster under the left arm of his coat and it immediately made me wary. Like everyone else, his attention focused on me. Harv must have sensed my discomfort as he quickly introduced me to Ralph Dixon, the Tansy Club owner, as *Mrs. LeDoux*. Ralph rested his hand on the back of my chair and smiled down at me. His slick, dark hair and thin mustache gave him the elegant look of a silent film star, but the intense gaze of his ebony eyes sent a chill down my spine.

"Mrs. LeDoux," he said smoothly, "welcome to the Tansy Club. If I may take the liberty of saying so, you look exceptionally lovely this evening."

"Thank you." I forced a smile and sat up straighter. I didn't like his fingers grazing my shoulder. Even though a fringed shawl covered most of my upper body, the light pressure of his hand made the goosebumps come back to my arms with a vengeance.

I wore a sleeveless, V-neck dress made from silk charmeuse in soft gold with hand-sewn beadwork along the neckline. The drop waist had a matching sash that tied in a generous bow on my right hip, drawing attention to a skirt embellished with several tiers of flounces. I'd worn it tonight because I wanted to look festive, but now I began to wonder if I should have shown up in widow's weeds and a veiled hat instead.

"Enjoy your dinner," Ralph Dixon said and moved on to visit with guests at another table. I immediately breathed a sigh of relief, but my reaction made me realize I wasn't quite ready for a night out on the town. Despite all the gaiety taking place around me, I felt lonely and out of place. Suddenly, all I wanted was to go home to my little family, slip into my soft, flannel nightgown and snuggle with my baby under the warm blankets on my bed.

My thoughts were cut short when our waiter appeared at our table to take our dinner order. Keeping my discomfort to myself, I smiled politely and decided on the breast of chicken a la rose, Waldorf salad, and potato croquettes. Maybe I was just hungry and tired, I reasoned. Maybe if I had a nice dinner and listened to the music for a while, my morale would improve.

12

As I waited for my appetizer of shrimp cocktail to arrive, I slowly sipped my wine, careful not to drink too much on an empty stomach. I hadn't had any alcohol in almost a year and didn't want to get ossified to the point where I embarrassed myself by knocking over my wineglass or dropping my silverware on the floor.

"Well, hello, there," a familiar male voice murmured over my shoulder. Surprised, I twisted in my chair to find Benny Howe, a man who used to be a regular customer at La Coquette and a good friend.

"Benny, how are you?" I smiled warmly, relieved to see someone I knew. "Are you here with your family?"

A lock of curly auburn hair fell across his forehead as he gazed down at me. "I heard the food and gambling here was the best in the Twin Cities—now that La Coquette is gone—so, me and a couple of guys decided to have steak for dinner and play a few hands at the tables downstairs."

Benny's family owned a jewelry store in downtown Minneapolis. He always had plenty of money to spend but proved to be the worst card player Gus had ever seen. According to my late husband, even a blind old lady could beat Benny at poker. Still, Gus liked him and always described him as a good *kid*, even though he was twenty-seven; two years older than me.

"This place is packed, Benny. How did you find me?"

"We were sitting at the bar when you came in." He gave me a toothy grin. "You're the only woman I know with your shade of dark brown hair and a fur coat that's bigger than you." He leaned close. "How have you been, Char?"

"I'm doing fine," I said, hoping he wouldn't ask about how I'd been coping with Gus' death or the demise of La Coquette. I didn't want to talk about my past. I wanted to move forward with my life.

His face bore a hopeful expression. "Would you like to dance?"

I glanced at the elbow-to-elbow situation on the dance floor and shook my head. "I don't think so—"

He took my hand and gave it an encouraging tug. "C'mon, Char. You look like you could use some cheering up. I'd be honored to be your partner. I know you're a terrific dancer."

I laughed at the compliment. "You're not so bad yourself!" Benny was an excellent dancer and the reigning champion of La Coquette's all-night dance marathons.

Marv heard what we were discussing and gave me a little nudge. "Go. Dance. Enjoy yourself."

The orchestra began to play "Yes, Sir, That's My Baby."

"C'mon!" Benny grabbed my other hand and pulled me to my feet before I had a chance to refuse. "Let's show this clip joint how to kick up some dust!" He drew me onto the dance floor and we eased our way into the crowd. The circular flounces on my skirt swished as we began to hop to the tune in perfect sync. Before long, Benny began to show off, circling me with his own version of fancy Charleston footwork. I stopped and doubled over with laughter, mainly to cover up the fact that not only was I out of breath but also out of shape for this much exercise. I hadn't danced like this since before I'd become pregnant.

The orchestra switched to the blues song "Easy Come, Easy Go" to cool down the crowd, and Benny gently pulled me into his arms. "I never got the chance to tell you how sorry I am about Gus," he said as he effortlessly guided me in a waltz. "I wanted to talk to you at the funeral, but you were surrounded by so many of Harv's people, I couldn't get close enough to get your attention. Besides, you looked deeply distracted."

If you only knew…

My eyes began to mist. I looked away to avoid showing the guilt that still plagued me over shooting another human being—even if it was in self-defense, but he placed his fingers under my chin and slowly turned my head. "Hey, I'm sorry. I didn't mean to make you cry."

I sniffled. "It's not your fault, Benny. I—"

"Let's talk about something more pleasant—like your eyes," he said as he locked gazes with me. "They're the most unusual color combination I've ever seen."

"How so?" I had never studied my eye color that closely but welcomed the topic change.

"Your green irises are etched with a blue ring around them. They're beautiful and unique. Just like you."

Okay, I thought, becoming uncomfortable again. *That's enough compliments. Pretty soon he's going to try to kiss me...*

There was no law against kissing someone, but I absolutely did *not* have any interest in getting romantically involved with Benny Howe or any of Gus' former associates. To his credit, Benny was polite, attractive, and a sweet fellow. As far as I was concerned, however, that's all he would ever be to me—a nice guy and a friend.

"Thank you for asking me to dance, Benny, but I'm getting tired and I'm starving. I'd like to go back to my table now." My mouth watered at the thought of the delicious shrimp cocktail waiting for me.

"Sure, Char." He couldn't hide his disappointment as he gently let go of my waist. "Whatever you say."

Suddenly, someone grabbed my hand and spun me around. "Well, well, look who we have here..."

I found myself staring into the ruggedly handsome face of Leonard Murtagh, one of Gus' former bodyguards. Leonard stood about five inches taller than me with short, dark hair combed straight back, gunmetal-blue eyes, and a dimple on his chin. Like Gus, he favored hand-tailored suits, Tommy guns, and fast cars. He could be quite charming when it suited him, but I knew he possessed a penchant for violence and I didn't want anything to do with him.

"My turn to dance with the little lady," Leonard said with an air of authority, dismissing Benny.

Who does he think he is, cutting in like I'm his property?

I glared into Leonard's eyes, only too happy to give this thug the bum's rush. "I'm not your little lady and *I* decide who I dance with, Leonard. Excuse me, my dinner is waiting." Benny's schoolboy crush on me made me uneasy, but Leonard's cavalier attitude toward his former boss' wife simply made me *mad*. I spun away to head back to my table.

"Hey, come back here." Laughing, he caught me by sliding his arm around my waist. "It's been a while since that afternoon in the alley, Charlotte," he whispered in my ear as he pressed my back to his chest. "You and me got some catching up to do."

I *did not* want to be reminded of the day Gus died. Gus had ordered Leonard to wait for us in the alley with the car so we could escape from the Feds. I didn't know what had happened to delay him, but Leonard wasn't there when we arrived. Perhaps if he had been on time, things would have turned out differently. In any case, it was too late for what-ifs, apologies, or excuses. Or to make amends. I pried his hands from my waist and wrenched myself away from him. "Let me go!"

Ignoring my hostility, he cocked one brow as his gaze swept over my body. "You've changed. Developed some spunk. Baby, you're the cat's meow."

"Yeah, well I'm one cat who's not looking for a new tom." I lifted my chin high. "I'm doing just fine on my own."

He laughed at my bold assertion as though I'd come up with the funniest joke he'd heard in a long time. "The man who tries to tame you is in for a wild ride."

Benny wedged himself between us. "Look, Murtagh, she doesn't want to dance with you so leave her alone."

Leonard stared hard at Benny as his hand reached inside his jacket. "Beat it, punk."

"Stop it, both of you," I snapped. "We're leaving. Come on, Benny." I slipped my arm around Benny's and tried to pull him away, but he ignored me. Both men stared at each other like rutting stags ready to lock horns. Things were going to get ugly for Benny if I didn't get him out of there fast.

Several men had elbowed their way through the crowd and stood behind Leonard in a show of force. I knew one of them, Earl Bauer, a small-time thief, and big-time jailbird. Earl had built a sordid reputation as a lounge lizard, among other things. He'd spent many nights at La Coquette, guzzling hooch and harassing everything in a skirt. Earl parted his dirt-brown hair in the center and slicked it back with so much Brilliantine hair oil his head looked like patent leather. His cheap three-piece suit and greasy skull were repulsive to me, but his ugly glower made it absolutely clear he was itching for a good fight. "One word, boss," he announced, "and we'll escort this bum out on a stretcher."

"Come on, Benny," I said, growing increasingly alarmed. I pulled on his arm again. "Let's *go*."

By now, most people had backed away, forming a wide circle around us. Four young men came up behind me and instinctively I knew they were Benny's chums.

Fear prickled at the back of my neck. I let go of Benny and backed into the crowd, ready to run. As the widow of a bootlegger who'd never backed down from a fight in his life, I knew what was coming, and I prayed gunfire would not be involved…

I didn't see who threw the first punch. I only knew that suddenly women were screaming, fists were swinging, overturned tables and dishes were crashing to the floor, and panicked people were fleeing to the exit. Within seconds, the entire room had erupted into total madness.

A large, strong hand gripped my arm. "Come with me, Char," a familiar masculine voice spoke loudly in my ear. "I'm getting you out of here."

I spun around and stared into a pair of deep blue eyes. "Will!" I was taken aback in surprise at the presence of the tall private investigator. "Where did you come from?"

Will Van Elsberg placed his broad hand between my shoulder blades and swiftly pushed me behind an overturned table, saving me from getting hit by a chair careening over our heads. "I've been here all along," he shouted through the deafening noise, "keeping an eye on the situation."

What did he mean by that?

I'd known Will since last May, a month after I'd left my husband and gone into hiding. Not knowing the truth about who I was, Will had hired me to work as his housekeeper and cook. When he eventually discovered my real identity—Gus LeDoux's missing wife—he'd risked his own life to protect me from Gus and then from the authorities. Needless to say, I trusted this man completely. This was not the first time he'd held my life in his hands, but I hoped it would be the last. I wanted nothing more to do with bootleggers!

"Will, let's go!" Daniel Blythe, Will's assistant, ran toward us and helped me to my feet. I knew Daniel as Will's handyman and home security guard, a jovial man who'd always worn denim coveralls and a newsboy hat. I wouldn't have recognized him tonight in a suit except for the thick, wiry mustache that matched his coppery hair. He shoved my beaded purse at me. "The brothers are getting your coat. We're supposed to meet them at the front door. C'mon!"

We ran toward the exit and eased our way through a stampede of people in the waiting area, trying to escape. Harv stood by the cloakroom door, holding my coat and cloche hat. He quickly slipped it over my shoulders and placed his hand on the small of my back, pressing me

18

forward to blend into the moving crowd. Will grabbed his fedora and shoved it over his thick black hair. He and Daniel shrugged into their long overcoats as they followed close behind.

When we finally made it outdoors, the road behind the barn looked like a parking lot, blocked with dozens of cars trying to get around the building and onto Highway 61. I looked around but couldn't locate the Katzenbaums' Rolls Royce in the sea of vehicles.

"Char, you go with Will. He can get you away from here faster than we can," Harv said and hugged me. "I'm sorry about tonight, honey. We'll make it up to you, I promise."

He turned to Will. "I'm trusting you to get her out of here safely and take her home. We'll talk tomorrow."

Will and Dan were both in their mid-thirties and in good physical shape. Flanking me, they gripped my arms to keep me from stumbling as we ran over the bumpy, frozen ground to their car. Daniel got the car started while Will helped me into the front seat and got in beside me. How in the world were we going to get past this conglomeration of automobiles?

Shots cracked through the air. The fight had taken a sinister turn.

"Time for a shortcut!" Daniel took off, driving like a lunatic as he raced across a snowy field. Warmer temperatures and sunny days had shrunk the snow cover considerably, but the ground was still frozen, creating a jarring ride. We eventually made it to the highway and took off into the night.

I let out a sigh of relief. "I'm never going back there again." Both men laughed. "I mean it," I protested and shook my head. "That place was full of criminals. Many of whom I knew on a first-name basis! I should never have let Benny talk me into getting on the dance floor. It was a prescription for disaster." I remembered how everyone had stared at me when we first arrived and the realization that Leonard had been one of them made me shiver.

"Are you cold?" Will reached into the back seat and grabbed a blanket. "Here, this should help," he said as he spread it over my lap. "It wasn't about you, you know."

I stared at him in the dark. "What do you mean?"

"There's a turf war going on right now," Daniel said, never taking his gaze off the road.

"Since Harv and Marv have taken over Gus' bootlegging territory," Will added, "some people feel the brothers are grabbing too much power."

"I know that, but the fight started over me."

Will turned his head. The cold, silvery moonlight streaked across the lean planes of his clean-shaven face. "It's *always* about power, Char."

Men fighting for territory and influence—I'd lived through more than my share of power struggles, but now that my husband was gone, I'd made myself a promise. I'd never go back to that dangerous and violent life again.

Chapter Two

The corner banquette at Stan's diner was wide and roomy with red leather seats. I sat between Will and Daniel, sipping hot chocolate and eating a frosted doughnut as I waited for my breakfast to be served. Eggs and toast were a far cry from shrimp cocktail or chicken a la rose, but it was ten o'clock in the evening and I was so hungry my stomach hurt. I was also extremely disappointed. My wonderful Saturday night out had turned disastrous.

"On the way here, you said the fight tonight was all about power," I stated, licking white frosting off my fingers. "Tell me what's going on." I glanced from Will to Daniel. "Why were you two at the Tansy Club at the same time I was there with the Katzenbaums? Did Harv hire you for extra protection?"

The thought that Harv would expose me to unnecessary danger didn't ring true. Harv was an extremely careful and thorough individual. The brothers wouldn't purposely put me in harm's way. They'd become the father I never had.

"No, we weren't on the clock," Will said, taking a sip of hot coffee. "I ran into Harv yesterday at a restaurant downtown. I asked about you and he mentioned taking you to dinner tonight. Given the present tension over Gus' territory, Dan and I decided to drop into the Tansy Club to keep an eye on things." He set down his cup. "One way to send a clear warning to the brothers that Murtagh and his gang mean business is to threaten you."

I dipped the last chunk of my doughnut into my hot chocolate. "Leonard came across as pushy and obnoxious, but he didn't verbally threaten me."

"He didn't need to. Approaching you on the dance floor sent Harv the message that he'll go to any length to get what he desires most."

I paused. "What's that?"

Will gave me an *"Are you serious?"* frown. "To be the next Gus LeDoux."

I almost laughed. *No one* would ever fill Gus' shoes. Gus had spent his entire youth working in his father's brewery and had learned how to successfully manage people. He'd used those skills to build his bootlegging empire. The moonshiners who did business with him looked up to him and were fiercely loyal. Given the way Leonard had acted tonight, he had a lot to learn if he ever hoped to become as successful as Gus.

Will had obviously suspected the brothers might run into trouble and had chosen—on his own—to monitor the situation as a precaution. Did he know something that Harv didn't? Or had Will made it his mission to watch over *me*?

"Leonard Murtagh is not a man to cross," Daniel said with a shake of his head as he picked up the glass sugar dispenser and poured a generous amount into his coffee.

Will held up his cup as a waitress passed by with a coffee pot. She stopped and gave the men steaming refills.

"When you started arguing with him on the dance floor, I figured we'd have to step in and diffuse the situation. When your dance partner's friends showed up, I knew things could escalate fast." Will reached up and brushed my cheek with his thumb. "Then it was a matter of getting you away before you got caught in the ruckus and got hurt."

Though I should have been grateful for his help, I quietly bristled with annoyance. What *nobody* seemed to realize was that I didn't need rescuing from Leonard Murtagh on the dance floor and I didn't need a self-appointed committee of men making my decisions for me. I was a modern woman! I wanted to make my own decisions!

I drank the last of my hot chocolate to calm my agitation. It didn't help. "How did you know Leonard would be at the Tansy Club tonight?"

Will gave me a stern look. "I'm a detective. That's my job."

In other words, it's none of your business, Char.

"You went to the Tansy Club last night to bribe the bartender into telling you that Leonard was a regular, didn't you?"

His mouth formed a tight line. "I never discuss my methods."

Our waitress appeared; her arms were laden with platters of piping hot food. My mouth watered as she set a plate of eggs and fried potatoes in front of me. I reached for the jam dish to smear strawberry preserves on my buttered toast and quietly went about eating my meal, but my mind continued to spin with questions.

Will was a good investigator and could be tough as nails when necessary. He and I were friends, though, and he normally didn't take such a hard line with me, giving me cause to wonder what else was going on. I understood the struggle for control of Gus' bootlegging territory. That was the way things evolved in that business. But was someone trying to get control of my legitimate businesses, too? If so, they were going to have a fight on their hands. Men like Leonard Murtagh and his henchman, Earl Bauer, were ruthless and violent, but I had been educated by *the best* man in the underworld and I had no intention of allowing anyone to take advantage of me.

Perhaps my fretting was an overreaction and I was simply making a mountain out of a molehill. But what if my suspicions were right? I didn't like being kept in the dark when it involved my safety or my future.

I didn't like it at all.

* * *

It was late by the time Will and Daniel brought me home. Francie had left the yard light on for me and it illuminated the sidewalk as Will walked me to the front door.

"Thanks for stopping at Stan's to get me something to eat," I said, pausing on the step, "and for bringing me home."

Melting snow from the roof had dripped onto the cement stoop and then refrozen, creating icy spots. My brocade T-strap shoes could easily slip on slick areas, causing me to take a tumble. Will slipped his arm around my waist to support me as he guided me up the steps. "I'm sorry the evening didn't work out tonight the way you had expected," he said solemnly.

"It wasn't a total loss, Will." I smiled. "We had breakfast together."

He laughed, the corners of his deep blue eyes crinkling. "If that was a date, I failed miserably."

I stopped at the door, not ready to go into the house yet. It had been a month since the last time I'd talked to him; specifically, the night Francie and I went to see a movie at the State Theater in downtown Minneapolis. During the intermission, I stood in the lobby waiting for Francie to come out of the ladies' room when he approached me. I knew then I wanted to see him again and I said as much to him. He told me—sincerely—that because I had my hands full with a sick mother and a new baby, he was willing to wait until my life settled down before he asked me out. Since then, not much had changed but I wanted him to know that I hadn't forgotten our discussion.

"Will, I…" I looked up. The desire in his eyes made my heart flutter. "Since the last time we spoke… I've been meaning to call you, but things haven't been going so well with Mamma and I've been overwhelmed with the baby and working with the brothers to learn how to manage Gus' businesses—"

"Hey, hey, it's okay," he said, his deep voice assuring me in a gentle, caring tone. "I understand. I really do. You've got your hands full right now. Don't worry about it."

I exhaled a deep sigh of relief. "Thank you. I didn't want you to think I'd changed my mind."

He flashed a broad smile. "I'd never think that." His dark brows furrowed. "There is one thing that bothers me, though. Lately, I've been worrying about it." The brim of his fedora, positioned at an angle on his head, cast a silvery shadow across his face. "This house doesn't provide much protection for you or your family…" He glanced around, assessing the area with a critical eye. "You're not safe here. Not right now, anyway. You need to move back into your place on Summit Avenue."

By "place" he meant the brick Richardsonian Romanesque mansion Gus had built for me. The estate had a vine-covered wrought iron fence surrounding the property and a guardhouse at the entrance. It provided plenty of security, but the loneliness of living in a secluded fortress had always given me the feeling of being locked in a gilded cage.

I shook my head. "My mother is too ill to withstand a change that drastic and I won't leave her again. Besides, she wouldn't consent to vacate her home even if I begged her—which I would *never* do."

He nodded with resignation, his expression grave. "Well, for now, the brothers will have security teams watching this house around the clock. I recognized one of their cars parked in the alley when we pulled up." He placed his hands on my shoulders and gently squeezed. "Promise me you'll be careful when you go out. You won't go anywhere without a bodyguard."

I hated the idea! I'd spent too many years being chaperoned everywhere by Gus' trained army and the thought of giving up my independence upset me. Will, however, wasn't anything like Gus and if he wanted me to cooperate with Harv's men, I knew it was because he was genuinely concerned about me and not trying to control every move I made. "All right," I replied reluctantly.

He glanced around again, sharply scanning the area. "You'd better go inside." The metal spring creaked as he pulled open the screen door. "Dan's keeping an eye on the street, but I don't think it's wise to stand out here too long." He twisted the knob on the wooden entrance door and pushed it open. A rush of warm air escaped from the living room, enveloping us like a soft blanket. He kissed my cheek and guided me firmly inside. "Lock your doors and windows. Goodnight."

I didn't get the chance to wish him goodnight before he pulled the door shut firmly in my face and headed back to his car. I stood in the shadows of the darkened living room and watched through the window as his tall, broad-shouldered silhouette walked down the sidewalk, wondering why no matter how much things changed, in some ways they always seemed to stay the same.

Like being shadowed by a couple of goons equipped with enough artillery to guard a castle.

I let out a tense breath. I thought that part of my life—the necessity for round-the-clock protection—had ended when my husband died. I posed no threat to Gus' rivals and had repeatedly made it known I wanted nothing more to do with that sector of society. So, why did I still find myself imprisoned by it?

I watched Will's car drive away and then sat on the sofa in the dark, brooding over my predicament. "I will *not* live like this anymore," I whispered angrily to myself. "I don't care how long it takes or what I have to do, I'm going to take control over my own life."

Chapter Three

"Happy birthday, dear Francie," I sang loudly to my sister. Julien wiggled in my arms as Mamma watched on. "Happy birthday to *you*!"

Francie laughed and clapped her hands. Julien ignored us all and rubbed his eyes. He needed to go down for his morning nap, but we wanted him to join the party for at least a little while. We'd set up the small table in Mamma's bedroom with a linen cloth and a frosted chocolate cake that Francie had picked out herself at O'Brien's bakery.

"Cut the cake, Francie, while I change Julien and lay him down." I walked over to where Mamma lay in bed, reclining against her pillows, and held the baby close to her. She'd been strangely quiet all morning. "Give Grandma a kiss," I said to my chubby-faced little boy. He was too young to understand, of course, but the gesture made Mamma smile. She kissed the tips of her fingers and shakily placed them on his forehead. The small movement seemed to take every ounce of strength she had.

After I changed Julien and wrapped him snuggly in a soft blanket and put him to bed, I returned to Mamma's bedroom with an envelope for Francie. "For you, sweetie." I handed it to her. "This is from me and Mamma. So, how does it feel to be fifteen?"

"It's exciting! I've been waiting *forever* to be this age!" Francie tore open the envelope. "Maybe I'll meet someone special this year like you did at my age."

I was fifteen when I met Gus, but Mamma and Papa wouldn't allow me to go anywhere alone with him until I'd turned sixteen. I used to stand outside the employee entrance of the LeDoux brewery on Friday afternoons at quitting time, waiting for Papa to finish his shift. When he came out, I'd beg him for what little money I could get for groceries. He usually only gave me a pittance so I had to work at Finnegan's Hotel to make sure we had enough to eat. I'd made it my mission to confront him on payday before he went to the saloon because he often spent most of his money in one night, buying rounds for all of his friends.

Occasionally, I'd see a tall, sandy-haired youth leaving the building. The handsome boy wore clothes a cut above the average worker's and would always give me a long look before going on his way. One day he stopped and introduced himself as the owner's son, René LeDoux Jr, but said everyone called him Gus, a shortened version of his middle name. Our fascination with each other was instantaneous. We met every Friday afternoon at the brewery to talk and before long, we fell in love. Once my parents allowed him to start courting me, things escalated and we were married the same year. Gus was twenty and I was sixteen.

I cringed inside at the thought of my sister becoming entangled with a boy at such a young age. She had many more options than I'd had and I was determined to see her life turn out better than mine did. Granted, I had inherited a fortune from my late husband, but it came at a steep price.

Francie pulled out the birthday card and flipped it open. Her eyes widened as she gasped in surprise. "Twenty-five dollars!" She gave Mamma a hug. "Thank you, Mamma." She wrapped her arms around me. "Thanks, Char." Then she pulled away and held up the money, beaming. "I can't wait to go shopping!"

Francie ran up to her bedroom to stuff the money in her purse as I sat on the chair next to Mamma's bed and visited with her.

"She's such a happy girl," Mamma said in a voice so weak her words came out as a whisper. "But she needs guidance. Promise me you'll keep her under your wing when I'm gone. She looks up to you, Char."

"I will, Mamma. I promise." I leaned over and straightened the blankets on her bed. "But I'm not worried about dealing with that anytime soon. You're going to be with us for a long time."

She gave me a knowing look that made my heart sink.

It was a little early for cake, but the morning seemed to be the best time for Mamma. She tired easily and we wanted to have the party before her favorite radio show "The Betty Crocker Cooking School of the Air" came on. We turned on the radio and ate our cake as we listened to Betty Crocker discuss the recipe of the day.

Mamma had only eaten a small bite of cake before she closed her eyes. I removed the plate from her lap and pulled up the covers then turned down the radio to a whisper. Her pale cheeks had taken on a slight flush and that worried me.

Francie had taken the day off from school to celebrate her birthday and as soon as she finished helping me gather the cake dishes, she grabbed her coat and boots from the closet. Apparently, the birthday money was burning a hole in her pocket.

"I'll be back by suppertime!" She flew out the door clutching her tiny purse stuffed with birthday cash and two six-cent tokens for streetcar fare.

I kept a watchful eye on Mamma all day. By the afternoon she had developed a cough and complained of chest pain. I called the nurse, who had a standing appointment to check on her twice a week and asked her to come to the house right away. By the time Mrs. Nugent arrived, Mamma had the chills, even though I had put an extra blanket on her and turned up the oil burner in the kitchen.

The stout, gray-haired woman examined Mamma and quickly left the room. "I need to call Dr. Manning. Where is your telephone?"

Frightened by her urgency, I ushered her into the living room where the black, candlestick telephone sat on a small drum table. Nervous and upset, I paced the floor, worrying about Mamma's worsening condition while Mrs. Nugent consulted with Dr. Manning.

"What is wrong with my mother?" I asked sharply as soon as Mrs. Nugent put the receiver back in its cradle.

"We'll wait until the doctor gets here," she replied with finality. "He'll examine Anna and determine a diagnosis."

I walked the floor, waiting for the doctor. Francie breezed through the kitchen door at five o'clock carrying several bags and wearing a new cloche hat. She held up the bags. "Wait until you see what I bought!"

"It's about time you got home," I said in a trembling voice.

She stared at me, confused. "What's wrong with you?"

I let out a tense breath, suddenly unable to hold back tears. "It's Mamma. She's taken a turn for the worse and I needed you here."

Still wearing her coat and boots, Francie dropped everything on the kitchen table and ran to the bedroom. Mrs. Nugent stopped her at the door. "Wait until the doctor arrives. Your mother mustn't be disturbed."

Francie began to argue but Mrs. Nugent swiftly spun her around by the shoulders and pushed her back into the kitchen. "Wait for the doctor. He'll be here soon."

Tears of frustration spilled down Francie's cheeks as she collapsed on a chair at the table. "Mamma must have something really wrong with her, so why can't I see her?"

I put my arm around her shoulder and gave her a sideways hug. "Mamma is very weak. If we go in to see her, she'll try to talk and she needs to conserve her strength. Mrs. Nugent is keeping a close watch over her until the doctor gets here."

"What's happened to her?"

"I don't know," I replied in a despondent voice as I stared at the closed door to Mamma's bedroom. The sad truth was I knew what was happening but couldn't bring myself to acknowledge it by putting it into words.

Francie still had her coat on and given the stifling heat in the kitchen, I wondered why she hadn't made any effort to take it off. Something about that new black hat she bought looked strangely out of place as well. I stared at her for a moment then blinked in shock.

Where were her beautiful blonde braids?

I gasped aloud. "Francie, what did you do to your hair?" Before she could stop me, I snatched the hat off her head. She'd had her hair cut in a boyish bob with a line of bangs skimming her eyebrows. The level sides were trimmed to points at her cheekbones. It looked terrific on her but I was already so stressed out that all I could focus on was her blatant disobedience. "What do you think you're doing? Mamma expressly said you could *not* get a flapper cut until you were sixteen!"

"I did it because it's not fair!" Francie's mouth formed a rebellious pout. "A lot of my friends are getting their hair cut and they're wearing makeup, too!"

A heavy fist pounded on the front door.

"We'll discuss this later," I whispered angrily, hoping Mrs. Nugent hadn't overheard our heated conversation.

I greeted Dr. Manning at the door and took his coat. He wore a rumpled suit and wire-rimmed glasses. His thinning white hair was combed straight back, curling at the nape of his neck. He and Mrs. Nugent spent a few minutes examining Mamma before he approached me in the kitchen. "I'm afraid Anna has pneumonia," the elderly gentleman said gravely. A gold tooth gleamed in the front of his mouth. "I'm very sorry. Given her present state of health, there isn't anything I can do to bring her through this."

"Why can't you take her to the hospital?" I demanded, desperate to keep her alive as long as possible.

"Her heart is failing rapidly. She's too ill to move."

The news hit me hard. "H—how many days does she have left?"

He gazed into my eyes with gentle compassion. "Possibly hours…"

Francie started to bawl. My eyes pooled with fresh tears. I could barely speak. "What do we do now?"

"Mrs. Nugent has agreed to stay on for as long as she is needed. In the meantime, she'll try to keep Anna as comfortable as possible. If you have a clergyman, I suggest you call him immediately." He stood aside. "You may see her now, but keep in mind she's very weak so she may not be able to speak."

Francie and I immediately went into Mamma's bedroom and gingerly approached her bed. She lay with her eyes closed, her breathing labored. I picked up her hand. It was limp. Her eyes fluttered, but she didn't appear to be fully conscious. Francie and I positioned our chairs next to her bed and sat in silence, taking turns holding her hand.

A few minutes later, I called Pastor Olson. He'd been retired for many years and was well into his nineties, but he still kept in contact with a few of the parishioners from his church. Rain or shine, he knocked on the door every Wednesday morning to pray with Mamma and give her communion.

Dr. Manning's assessment sadly proved correct. Mamma never regained consciousness and a few minutes after two in the morning, she passed away. I understood very little about such things, but even so, when the gurgling in her chest went silent, I knew she had left us.

Francie had fallen asleep with her head and shoulders resting on the edge of the bed. Mrs. Nugent had gone to the kitchen with Pastor Olson to make a fresh pot of coffee. I sat in the softly lit room and stared at my mother's peaceful, heart-shaped face. She had no more pain.

What will I do without her? All my life, she has been my rock, my anchor. Her frailty made me strong...

I always knew this day would come, but nothing I had experienced, not even Gus' death, could have prepared me for this moment. I sat at her bedside, numb with grief and shock, feeling utterly alone.

*   *   *

Time and time again, my life had proven to be anything but normal, sane, or dull. I had hoped that one day things would settle down so I could raise my son in a safe, stable atmosphere. Unfortunately, Mamma's funeral didn't prove to be that day.

The organist played a nondescript hymn as I stood at the front of the church with Julien in my arms and received visitors to Mamma's wake. Holding the wake and funeral in her small home would have been inconvenient. Besides, I could afford something much better for her so I arranged for it to be held in the church where she'd been baptized as a child and years later, held her wedding. For her casket, I'd ordered a huge multi-colored spray of carnations, lilies, and gladiola, her favorite flowers. I'd hired a caterer to furnish a luncheon in the basement following her interment in the cemetery behind the building.

Beside me, Francie stood clutching her handkerchief, sobbing and hiccupping inconsolably. Harv and Marv stood beside us, silent and respectful. Will and Daniel had volunteered to be pallbearers along with four of Harv's bodyguards. A group of Mamma's neighbors arrived at the beginning of the wake and after viewing her body, sat in the pews quietly awaiting the service.

The next person to show up with plenty of security in tow was Leon Goldman, one of St. Paul's most successful and notorious gangsters. Of medium height and dark hair, his penchant for expensive suits and aura of confidence attracted women to him like a magnet. He had a pretty wife and several small children, but honoring his marital vows didn't appear to be a priority for him. His reputation as a womanizer preceded him only by his status as an accomplished "wheeler-dealer" in the underworld.

Leon's presence surprised me, although he had good reason to attend. His mother had worked side by side with Mamma at the same dressmaker's shop on the east side of St. Paul for a decade and they were the best of friends. Rose Goldman wasn't with him today and I worried that perhaps she had taken ill.

Oddly enough, however, Leon had a young man accompanying him that I guessed to be about seventeen and I assumed he'd brought his younger brother. One thing appeared painfully obvious; the youth didn't want to be there. He stared at the ground wearing a petulant frown and refused to speak to anyone.

The one person who should have made an appearance, but decided to forego the honor was none other than my father, Floyd Johnson. I had no idea where he lived or if he was still breathing, but I had published Mamma's obituary in the paper in the hope that he'd see it.

Leon approached me, his paid muscle watching his back, and immediately I sensed the tension rolling off the people around me like waves of electricity. Will and Daniel moved in behind me. Behind them were Harv's bodyguards.

Leon focused on me exclusively, as though we were the only two people in the room. "I'm sorry for your loss, Charlotte." His voice, though smooth and polished, held a note of genuine empathy.

"Thank you, Leon. I appreciate your concern."

He nodded. "Anna was a good woman. She will be deeply missed."

Francie burst into loud sobs.

Leon pulled the silk handkerchief from his suit pocket and offered it to her.

"This is my sister, Mary Francis." I shifted Julien in my arms. He was getting heavy. "And who is this?" I gestured toward the young man standing off to one side. I wanted to get our introductions over with so I could sit down.

Francie stopped crying and stared wide-eyed as if noticing the youth for the first time.

"It's my nephew, Elliott Cohn. My sister's boy. He's staying with me for the rest of the school year while his parents are cavorting across Europe." Leon gave Elliott a nudge forward. "Elliott! Where are your manners? Introduce yourself to the ladies."

"Hi," Elliott said in a monotone voice without looking up, giving the impression he found the attention a form of punishment. "It's nice to meet you. I'm sorry for your dead person—" He darted a frightened look at his disapproving uncle. "…er—I mean…your loss.

Francie let out a loud sniffle, causing Elliott to shoot a guilty look our way. He and Francie exchanged glances before his face flushed bright crimson and he resumed staring at his shoes.

"How is your mother doing," I inquired to Leon, anxious to change the subject. "I hope Rose is well."

"She's battling a cold right now and sent me in her place."

The dark tone of his voice gave me the feeling he had an alternative motive for showing up, but I didn't say so. Perhaps he wanted to see for himself if the gossip about the brothers taking me under their wings was true. Or, was it because I'd been observed leaving the Tansy Club on the arm of a certain private detective? Whatever the case, I didn't like the idea that he was checking up on me.

Leon scanned the sparse crowd in the pews. "Where's Floyd?"

It was my turn to flush with embarrassment. "I don't know. I haven't heard from Papa in months."

Leon looked surprised. "Would you like him to be here?"

"For Mamma's sake, yes."

Leon snapped his fingers and one of his bodyguards silently appeared at his side like an obedient Doberman. He whispered something in the man's ear and then turned back to me. "I'll see what I can do."

Good luck, I thought. It was a thoughtful gesture on Leon's part, but probably a waste of time. "Thank you," I replied in an effort to sound hopeful even though I didn't believe it would happen.

Will's lips suddenly brushed my ear. "The minister would like to speak to you."

I spoke briefly with Pastor Olson then Francie and I took our places in the front pew of the church to signal the service was about to start. At my insistence, Will sat next to me with Francie on my right. He slid his arm behind me, across the back of the pew, and kept it there for most of the service.

Toward the end of the minister's sermon, a commotion erupted in the back of the church. Julien had fallen asleep on my lap so I turned slowly to see what was going on and my mouth dropped open as I recognized my father being forcefully seated in the last pew by one of Leon's burly henchmen. I winced at Papa's filthy, disheveled appearance. He looked like he'd been living in a hog pen.

I turned back toward the front and stared at Mamma's casket, so humiliated and ashamed I wished I could slide under the pew. I looked at Francie to gauge her reaction and caught her staring at Elliott. This time Elliott had found the nerve to stare back.

My worst fear had just been confirmed. Francie's new hairstyle and makeup had given her the "look" she wanted to be popular with her peers, especially boys. No wonder Mamma had been so adamant about

Francie refraining from such things until she'd turned sixteen. Hopefully, by that time, she'd have gained the maturity to handle the attention she was bound to receive. Mamma hadn't even been buried yet and I had already failed her where Francie was concerned.

I let out a defeated sigh. Between the uninvited gangsters, rebellious youths, and my drunken father, Mamma's funeral had all the makings of a three-ring circus.

I prayed it didn't end like my visit to the Tansy Club.

Chapter Four

After the interment, everyone congregated in the basement for a buffet-style lunch. And of course, a few discreet nips of hooch to round out the occasion. Other than the sip of wine at dinner two weeks ago, I hadn't had a drink in well over a year, but given the circumstances, I found myself considering it. I just wanted to get through this day without any more pain.

Will set a plate of food in front of me and sat down next to me at the round table reserved for family. "I've fixed you a plate."

I couldn't do it myself because Julien was still sleeping. Will slid his arm along the back of my chair. His thoughtfulness was the only bright spot in my day.

"That was sweet of you, Will, but I don't think I can eat a thing. I'm too stressed."

He picked up a fork and scooped up a small mound of glorified rice. "You really should eat. You need to keep your strength up," he said with concern in his eyes as he placed the fork to my lips. I gave in and did as he asked. The sweet, creamy rice-pineapple-whipped-cream combination tasted heavenly and it made me realize I hadn't eaten a thing all day. Will had also selected potato salad and a ham sandwich made with a croissant for me. Suddenly hungry, I took the fork from his hand

and started to eat.

Since Francie was the only family I had, I'd invited Will, Daniel, Harv, and Marv to sit at my table. I didn't see Papa anywhere in the room and assumed that Leon's men had already taken him back to the flophouse—or saloon—wherever they'd located him. I was still brooding over it when my nostrils were assaulted with the overwhelming odors of booze, stale cigarettes, and old sweat, proving me wrong.

"Hey, there, Charlie," Papa's voice rang out behind me. "Aren't you going to ask your papa to sit down? I'm family, too."

Slowly, I twisted in my chair and faced my father, Floyd Johnson, as he stood holding a plate piled high with food. He wore dark trousers and a grimy white shirt, but someone had obviously marched him into the lavatory and made him wash his face and hands, and comb his hair.

Daniel jumped out of his chair and grabbed his plate. "He can sit here. I'll go and join Harv's men."

Will started to rise from his chair to move over and allow Papa to sit next to me, but I grabbed his arm and shook my head. I couldn't deal with my father's disrespect toward his late wife or his nauseating odor right now. After an awkward moment, Will sat back down and indicated for Papa to take Daniel's chair.

I smiled at Daniel and thanked him for giving up his seat, but I was also grateful to have Will as a buffer between me and Papa. After the fuss Papa had caused at Gus' funeral, showing up at the last minute and shamelessly begging for money, I wondered what he had up his sleeve this time. I didn't want to find out.

"I see ya let Francie cut her hair and paint her face like a cheap doxie. She's shamin' our family!" Papa shoveled in forkfuls of potato salad between his grumblings. He'd lost more teeth since I'd last seen him and I had a difficult time understanding him at first. "If your Mamma was still alive, she'd never have allowed it but I 'spose now the two of ya think can do whatever ya please!"

Francie didn't appear to misunderstand him—not a single word. She stood up in a huff, threw her napkin on the table, and stomped away. I tried to call her back, but she kept going. My cheeks face flamed with fury at the hurt and embarrassment my father's callousness had caused my sister.

Papa picked up his sandwich and bit off half of it. "I'll be movin' into the house tonight and straightenin' out this family once and for all."

Not a word of condolence from him. Not a single question about Mamma or expression of grief. And yet, he assumed he was entitled to Mamma's property simply because he was her husband? He didn't know that it had never been in her name. Gus and I bought her that house. It was in *my* name.

Everyone at the table fell silent. Except me.

"How dare you..." My temper was on the verge of boiling over when Will's arm pressed against my back. At the same time, Harv grabbed my hand. I knew they were trying to calm me by being supportive, but at this point, nothing could slow the angry pounding of my heart. It was time for me to take my leave before I said something that would embarrass us all.

I had no intention of allowing Papa to move in with me. If he followed his usual pattern, he'd stay long enough to go through the house and pilfer everything of value he could carry before he disappeared again. If I had to, I'd pay to put him up somewhere, but he wasn't getting anywhere near my family.

I needed to find Francie, but I didn't know where she'd gone. I glanced across the room and saw her leaning against the wall with her arms folded. She looked hurt and alone. I didn't blame her. I knew exactly how she felt.

I kissed Harv on the cheek. "I need to get Julien home before he wakes up and starts fussing. Will you and Marv stay and thank everyone for coming? I'll call you later."

Harv gave me a concerned look. "Why are you leaving so soon? Floyd should be the one to go, not you. All he has done is upset you and your sister. If he were my relative, I'd have him thrown out on his ear." Harv rarely took a dislike to anyone, but I knew he hated my father for abandoning my mother.

"Francie wants to go home," I said, motioning toward her.

I turned to Will. "May I bother you for a ride?" I swallowed hard. "We need to go. *Now*."

Will nodded gravely and pushed back his chair.

Shifting the baby in my arms, I stood up and glanced across the room. Leon's nephew had approached Francie. Elliott said something to her and cupped her face in his hands. I knew he was trying to console her because she burst into tears. Before I could push my chair back to go after her, Elliott led Francie toward the stairway.

"I'll be right back," Will said in my ear. He stood up, pushed in his chair, and went after them, but he wasn't quick enough to catch Francie before she left the room.

I watched in dismay as Francie and her new friend disappeared into the stairwell and out of sight.

*   *   *

Early April

"Francie, welcome to your new home!"

As we entered my house on Summit Avenue, my sister grabbed her skirt and happily skipped the length of the hundred-foot reception hall embellished with hand-carved oak woodwork and cut-glass chandeliers. Straight ahead, the grand staircase, flanked by thick, Doric columns, led up to a wide landing where it divided into two staircases, one to the right and one to the left, both leading to the second-floor hall. Multiple windows with etched glass spread across the back wall, filling the airy, two-story space with soft, natural light.

We'd spent the prior week closing up Mamma's house. I had already hired a professional to sell the property and planned to turn over the proceeds to Marv to put in a trust account for Francie. She could have the money when she turned twenty-one.

"I've always loved this house, Char! Now that you're back living here, are we going to hold fancy dinner parties in the dining room?" Francie pointed to a large room at the end of the hall. Handcrafted sconces in the form of calla lilies embellished the wide doorway. "And dress up?"

"Maybe someday," I said patiently. The question made me pause. All of my old friends were either connected to bootlegging or were crooked coppers and I had no interest in seeing any of them again much less rolling out the red carpet for them at my house. I needed to make some new friends.

"I can't wait to invite the girls from school to stay overnight. I'm going to live here forever!" Laughing with delight, Francie ran up the stairs to claim one of the bedrooms on the second floor.

After Gus' death, I'd continued to employ a skeleton crew on the premises to keep the residence and grounds maintained and to discourage thieves from breaking in. Once I decided to move back, additional staff had been added, including a nanny for Julien. The servants, old and new, met us at the front door, welcoming us and taking our coats.

Gerard, my butler, pointed to the small mountain of suitcases in the entryway. "Shall I take your bags upstairs to your old room or will you be occupying the master bedroom?"

The thought of sleeping in Gus' wide bed without him seemed strange and unsettling to me. "I'll stay in my old room for now," I said quickly and handed off Julien to his new nanny, a short, redheaded young woman named Gretchen.

"Very good, My Lady." Gerard was a stout man in his mid-fifties, with dark hair, brown eyes, and stately manners. He had immigrated to

America from England several years ago. I loved the deep, melodious rumble of his voice and the formality of his British accent when he called me "*My Lady*."

I went upstairs to the third floor with Gretchen to inspect Julien's nursery and talk briefly about his daily schedule. Then I met up with Gerard in the east wing of the second floor in the adjoining bedrooms I used to share with Gus. After Gerard set down the bags in my room, he turned to me. "I have taken the liberty of ordering coffee for you. Dinner is served at seven."

Once he left, I sat on my four-poster bed, absently listening for Gus' booming voice before I realized my error. I sighed. Without Gus, the house had an empty, hollow feel to it. Had I made the right choice in moving back here? According to my inner circle, very much so, but they didn't have to live with the memories associated with this house like I did.

When my coffee arrived, I took my steaming cup and went across the hallway to Gus' study while my maid, Lillian, unpacked my suitcases. For some odd reason, Gus had insisted on converting one of the bedrooms into an office and I always wondered if he had a superstition about being on the first floor. His office at La Coquette had been located on the second floor as well.

The room had a large mahogany desk in the center with a candlestick telephone, brown leather upholstered chairs, and one solid wall of bookcases. Faint aromas of tobacco and Gus' bold cologne still lingered on the furniture and his desk blotter. Curious, I pulled open a drawer, surprised it wasn't locked. I expected to see a loaded gun or bundles of the supposed stash of cash Gus was rumored to possess, but all I found was his personal phone book. A medium-sized black book with tattered pages.

A wave of nausea crawled up the back of my throat. Upset, I slapped the book shut and forcefully closed the drawer. I didn't want to read the names and phone numbers of all the women my husband once knew—in the biblical sense.

Leaving Gus' study, I shut the door behind me and went in search of Francie, wondering which room she'd chosen to occupy. Each of the two wings in the house contained four bedrooms, and each bedroom had an adjoining bathroom, so no matter which one she chose, she would have complete privacy.

I found her new fringed handbag lying on a bed in the corner room of the west wing—as far as possible from my room. Her suitcases were sitting just inside the door. Francie, on the other hand, was nowhere to be found so I curiously went in search of her. I wanted to find out if she needed a snack to tide her over until dinnertime. *I* certainly did.

I found her downstairs in the library on the telephone. She had her back to the door so she didn't see me walk in.

"Elliott, it's me, Francie," she whispered. "I'm calling from my sister's house. Yeah, we moved in today. Golly, I'd forgotten how ritzy this place is, but the best part is that it has telephones everywhere and it's *so* big, no one will know when I'm on the line, much less overhear our conversations. I can call you anytime I want. Yeah, isn't that great? Hey, when can I see you again?"

I folded my arms and cleared my throat. Francie's jaw dropped as she whirled around and caught the deliberate frown of disapproval on my face.

She let out a huff. "Sorry, Elliott. Char's here. Gotta breeze. I'll call you later. Bye." She slammed the phone down. "You were spying on me! What gives you the right—"

"Francie, girls your age do not call boys! It's improper!" I didn't mean to yell or come across as high-handed, but that was how my response sounded.

"Maybe girls *your age* don't think it's proper, but all my friends *do*." She stormed past me. "I thought it was going to be fun living here. Guess I was wrong!"

I watched her stomp upstairs wondering what to do about her sudden, rebellious struggle against my authority. I winced with guilt, knowing how upset Mamma would be right now by Francie's behavior. And how badly I'd handled it.

Of all the boys in the world she could have befriended, why did she have to pick the close relative of a gangster? I shivered at the thought. I couldn't allow Francie to get mixed up with Leon Goldman's nephew. I didn't want her to spend the rest of her life looking over her shoulder, wondering if the Feds were on her tail, struggling with her husband's infidelities, and worrying when he left the house whether it would be the last time she saw him alive. I wanted my sister to meet a normal kid and have a normal marriage.

Sadly, I didn't want Francie's life to emulate mine.

Chapter Five

The next Monday morning, I resumed my training with the brothers. I needed to learn all aspects of running the businesses I took over for my late husband. I'd made arrangements with Harv to come into their office for a few hours every day during the week for instruction. Harv and Marv always sent a car to pick me up, but from now until the end of the school year, Francie and I would ride together. Francie didn't want to change schools so she needed to be dropped off at school each day.

The chauffeur dropped me off at the entrance to the Hamm Building in downtown St. Paul at seven-thirty. I wasn't expected at the office until eight o'clock, but Francie had to be at school by eight as well, so I volunteered to be dropped off first.

"Bye, Francie. See you tonight," I said as the chauffeur opened the door for me. When she didn't answer, I looked back and found her staring into a small mirror as she fussed with her makeup. Gripping my small leather briefcase, I extended a hand to the chauffeur to assist me. I gracefully alighted from the vehicle and walked across the busy sidewalk to the wide front doors of the building. As I approached, a young woman timidly came toward me wearing a thin, tattered coat and carrying a small tin in her gloveless hands.

"Spare some change, miss?" Her teeth chattered with each word as she held out the empty, battered can.

I stopped, taken aback by the desperation in her wide, brown eyes. Her dark hair rippled in the chilly breeze. She looked cold and hungry. And absolutely alone. She couldn't have been any older than my sister. Where was her family? Why had they abandoned her?

"Please?"

"Just a moment…" I said and opened my handbag to give her some money, feeling guilty for hesitating.

"Hey! You! *Beat it!*"

The girl suddenly gasped and ran away.

"Wait! I have your—" I held up a crisp five-dollar bill as I watched her disappear around the corner of the building.

"Don't do that, ma'am."

I spun around to confront the owner of the harsh voice and found myself staring at a uniformed policeman. "Why not?" I glared at him. "Why did you chase her away?"

He stared down at me, his gray eyes cold and unflinching. "You start giving handouts to bums on the street and pretty soon you'll have a dozen of them hanging around, pestering people and creating a nuisance." He pointed to the bill in my hand. "Put your money away."

"She was just a girl! And she was hungry. Don't you have a beating heart behind that badge?" I demanded as he arrogantly walked away, letting me know he didn't care what I had to say about the matter.

"If you want to help, give your money to the soup kitchen." He didn't even bother to turn his head as he lectured me.

Disgusted and shaken, I continued through the doors into the Hamm Building and walked across the lobby to a small, crowded café. I needed to sit down and get a cup of coffee to mull over what just happened.

I slid into a small booth set with two coffee cups and set my briefcase beside me on the seat. A waitress approached me right away carrying a coffee pot and a small menu card. She offered me the menu and asked if I wanted coffee.

"Just coffee. I've already had breakfast." Instead of looking at her, I concentrated on pulling off my gloves. I didn't want her to see me blinking away angry tears.

She turned over the cup sitting in front of me and filled it.

"Thank you." After she left, I slipped out of my coat and folded it neatly, placing it next to me in the booth. My cloche hat stayed on my head to avoid messing up my hair. I sipped the rich, black liquid and let out a deep, troubled sigh. Staring at my coffee cup, I became absorbed in my thoughts.

"Good morning."

Recognizing the deep, sensual voice, I looked up in surprise. My day had just improved one hundred percent. "Will…what are you doing here? Isn't your office on the other side of downtown?"

He stood gripping his black Fedora. "On a recommendation from Harv, Peter and I moved our office here a week ago. We were pretty cramped in our old space."

Will shared office space with an attorney by the name of Peter Garrett. Will handled investigations for Peter's cases, but he also took on cases independently. Now that they had Daniel Blythe working for them as well, they must have needed to make room for him.

"Are you meeting with the Katzenbaum brothers today?" he asked.

"Yes," I said, "they're instructing me on how to manage Gus' businesses. I'll be meeting with them every day until they feel I'm ready to handle things on my own."

His blue eyes shone like polished sapphires against his wavy black hair. "May I join you?"

I nodded and sat patiently as he dropped a folded copy of the *St. Paul Pioneer Press* on the table and then unzipped his jacket. He hung his hat and jacket on the coat hook fastened to the post at the end of the booth and slid in. As his gaze rested upon me, Will's wide, carefree smile faded quickly. "You look upset. What's wrong?"

"I just witnessed an unsettling incident."

The sharp, manly scent of his cologne wafted across the table. "What happened?"

The waitress appeared again before I had a chance to tell him. "Hi, Will," she said with a coy smile. "Would you like your usual breakfast today?" Her sickly-sweet voice made me glance up and I saw a pretty young woman with golden-brown hair trimmed just below her ears, parted on the side with finger waves.

Will smiled broadly. "Good morning, Iris. How are you?" He turned over his coffee cup and placed it back in the saucer. "Yes, thanks."

Iris batted her long eyelashes, heavily coated with black mascara, as she poured the hot coffee into his cup. Her cupid's bow lips shone with dark red lipstick. "Whatever you say, Will," she said with a breathy overtone.

I cleared my throat.

"Thanks," he said to her and turned his attention back to me. "Sorry about that." He reached across the table and took my hand in his. The gentle strength of his fingers intertwining with mine made my breath catch in my throat. "Tell me what happened."

I recounted in detail my chance encounter with the desperate young woman and the callous treatment she'd received from the officer. "She didn't do anything wrong. Being hungry and poor isn't a crime. He didn't have to treat her like that."

"It's a sad situation all around, but there's nothing you can do about it," Will said gently.

"You don't understand, Will." I took a sip of coffee and set down my cup. "Growing up, I could have easily turned out like that girl. You have no idea how poor my childhood was. I was raised in Swede Hollow in a shack with no electricity or running water. My mother was an invalid and my father was a drunk. I could have struck out on my own to escape the misery, however, all it would have taken was one mistake to find myself in dire straits like that poor girl." He already knew most of what I'd just told him, but I thought it was necessary to remind him of it to make him realize why the girl's situation had so profoundly affected me.

"But you didn't give up on your family," he said proudly. "You got a job at a hotel and took care of your mother."

"You mean, I got *lucky*." I sat back and folded my arms. "It was fortunate that I married a brewer's son who had both money and a willingness to support the women in my family. Honestly, I'm grateful that Gus left me well off, but you and I both know things could have easily gone the other way as they did for Mamma." I let out a troubled sigh and took another sip of coffee. "I know what you're getting at, Will, but I guess the real reason my nerves are on edge is that Francie is having growing pains and I don't know how to handle it."

Will gave me a puzzled look.

"She used her birthday money to get her hair cut even though she knew Mamma wouldn't allow it until she'd turned sixteen. Now she's wearing makeup and chasing after boys, too." I rolled my eyes. "Well, one in particular."

He laughed. "Isn't that normal for a girl her age?"

"Yeah, but the boy she's currently getting chummy with is Leon Goldman's nephew, Elliott Cohn. You know, the boy she met at Mamma's funeral. I know she's kept in touch with him because I caught her sneaking a call on the telephone to him. Now that we're living in *my* house, with telephones everywhere, she can slip into a room on the main floor, close the door and call him anytime she wants to." I shoved my coffee cup away. "Oh, Will, my sister *cannot* get mixed up with that family. I want her to go to college and marry a doctor—or anyone with a bright future ahead of him. I want my sister to have a wonderful life with a devoted husband, but it won't happen if she marries a bootlegger." I spit out the word *bootlegger* like it was my favorite swear word.

Iris sauntered over to our table and chatted with Will again as she refilled our coffee cups.

"Order up!"

She smiled and glanced toward the serving window. "Your breakfast is ready. I'll be right back." I watched her saunter away, her hips swaying for all to see, especially Will.

"So, you moved into the building last week, huh?" I gripped my coffee cup with both hands as I watched Iris grab a plate from the serving window. "It sure didn't take you long to get friendly with the locals."

He winked at me and smiled as Iris reappeared and set a plate of scrambled eggs and toast in front of him. She slipped a bottle of Heinz Ketchup from the pocket of her apron and set it on the table. "Would you like anything else?"

I almost snorted coffee through my nose.

He smiled at her. "I'm good. Thanks."

Iris walked away looking disappointed.

I watched him grab the ketchup bottle and unscrew the cap. "Don't tell me you're going to dump that on your breakfast."

He chuckled. "Want a taste?"

I began to laugh. "Ah...noooo." I glanced at a large round clock on the wall and grabbed my briefcase. "It's ten minutes to eight. I'd better get going." I slid out of the booth and reached across the seat for my coat.

Will's fork, heaped with eggs and ketchup, froze in midair. "Meet you here again tomorrow? Same time?"

"Okay," I said, slinging my navy wool coat and scarf over my arm. The thought of seeing him again spread a warm feeling across my chest. "Seven-thirty." I smiled. "I'll see you then."

I went to place a couple of coins on my guest check, but Will snatched it away. "I've got this."

"Thanks for the coffee. Have a good day." I headed for the elevator to go up to the brothers' office on the sixth floor. The weather outside hadn't changed, but the sun had begun to shine on my gloomy mood. I had something to look forward to tomorrow and I planned to be there early.

*   *   *

"Good morning, Char." The deep wrinkles in Marv's face crinkled as he welcomed me into his crowded office with pebble glass windows and the nose-wrinkling odor of stale cigarettes. His gravelly voice sounded especially rough today. I glanced at his Camel cigarette burning in a round glass ashtray on his cluttered desk, piled high with folders and stacks of opened envelopes, and hoped it wouldn't accidentally ignite the entire mess on fire. Seemingly oblivious to the possibility, Marv coughed and picked up his coffee mug. "Ready to get started? We've got a lot of work to do on the accounts today."

Marv started my training by teaching me the basic principles of accounting. Now I was working on the accounts of my Ford dealership—payables and receivables, payroll, and inventory. The bookkeeper at the dealership had retired a couple of months ago, and we fully anticipated hiring another one, but for now Marv wanted me to learn how to become proficient at it so I could properly manage every facet of that business myself. The dealership wasn't the only business I owned, but it was the largest and most profitable.

I should have learned how to do this back when I managed La Coquette, but Gus had always handled the bookkeeping responsibilities and any decisions dealing with the finances. He insisted I had enough on my hands handling the staff, the entertainment, and everything in between.

Learning how to manage every aspect of my businesses gave me a feeling of empowerment and independence. The more I learned, the more I wanted to know. Never again would I depend upon someone else to take care of me—or to make decisions for me.

I was determined to take full control of my destiny.

In the afternoon, I started working with Harv, learning how to manage all of Gus' rental properties. We sat together at his conference table and he pulled a handful of pages from a manila folder. Harv's thick gray brows furrowed as he squinted through his rimless spectacles at something on the top sheet.

"This is a complete list of all the properties you own," he said, placing the sheet on the table in front of me. "I had this typed up for you."

Wide-eyed, I picked up the sheet and studied it carefully. I had no idea Gus owned so much property or when he had purchased any of it. Why had he kept so much vital information from me? Perhaps he hadn't done it intentionally. I had been so busy managing La Coquette that I hadn't had time to get involved with anything else and he may have simply put it off.

To my surprise, I owned a dozen farms in Morrison and Stearns counties. I pointed to them. "Why did Gus buy up a bunch of farms? He knew nothing about farming."

Harv peered at me through his spectacles. "Yes, but he knew all about selling himself to ordinary people. Gus acquired every one of these properties through foreclosure auctions. He allowed the farmers to stay in their homes and helped them to set up stills to make moonshine that they, in turn, sold to him."

I gasped. "Are all of these farmers still making moonshine on my properties?"

Harv stared at me over the top of his spectacles. "Why, yes, of course."

"Who are they selling it to now?"

He gave me a baffled look. "You're well aware that Marv and I took over Gus' bootlegging operation."

"...but...but...it's illegal to own and operate a still. I didn't know you were involving my tenants in your business."

Harv clasped his hands on the table and gave me a hard look. "How else would these people make a living out in the sticks?"

Now it was my turn to be baffled. "Shouldn't they be farming?"

Harv sighed. "Dear woman, since the war ended prices for agricultural products have fallen so low it's difficult for farmers to survive. Many are going bankrupt. That's what happened to all of the acreages Gus purchased and that's why many farmers have turned to a new industry. By looking the other way, you're helping them to keep food on their tables and clothes on their backs."

"But, Harv—"

"Look," he said and placed his hand over mine, "we need to visit all of these locations so you can meet the tenants. You need to view each property anyway so you know what you own."

I persisted with my argument, but once again he cut me off.

"You can talk to all of your tenants about their situations, and if you aren't convinced that what they're doing is right, we'll have to make some other arrangements."

I didn't know what that meant, but I assumed the brothers would simply purchase the properties from me. "All right," I conceded, though I knew I wouldn't change my mind. I didn't want anybody *makin' moon* on my properties.

"Good," Harv replied emphatically. "We'll set it up. Now that the snow is nearly gone and the days are getting longer, it should make for a nice trip."

With that settled, I scanned the rest of the list. Most of the addresses were described as rental properties—some residential and some commercial—but near the bottom were a half-dozen soda shops. My jaw fell when I saw the name *Big Louie's* among them. How many times had I visited Big Louie's soda shop last summer when I was on the run from Gus, working as Will's housekeeper? What if Gus had made a surprise visit while I sat in a booth eating ice cream? The thought made my stomach leap.

I looked up. "Gus owned soda shops? What on earth for?" The moment the words left my lips a startling thought answered the question for me. "Harv, I hope you're not operating blind pigs in the back rooms of my ice cream parlors. Those shops cater to families!"

A "blind pig" was a small saloon operating in a building where the façade of a legitimate business was used as a cover. In my case, the legitimate business was real, but I'd heard of shops storing liquor bottles under the soda fountain to "jazz" up certain drinks.

"No, no." Harv held up his hands. "Gus merely used the back rooms as storage space for his goods. We've moved everything to new locations." He shook his head. "Somebody has been breaking into those shops looking for something and helping themselves to our stock at the same time. I don't know what they're trying to find, but whatever they wanted that belonged to Gus, they didn't find it there."

Really? That comment made me ponder the "secrets" rumor again for a moment. Who would have had firsthand knowledge of Gus' private dealings? Not just day-to-day stuff, but the kind of information only a few people who were acquainted with him intimately would know? The people closest to Gus were his inner circle—of course. There was just one problem. Except for Leonard Murtagh, every one of them was dead. Slain in a shootout with the Feds on the same day Gus was killed. So, who was breaking into my soda shops, and what did they want? Was it Leonard or someone else?

I didn't have a clue, but—somehow—I needed to find out.

Chapter Six

The next morning, I walked into the café at twenty minutes after seven, only to find Will already sitting in the same booth, waiting for me. The moment our gazes met a surge of elation filled my heart. "Good morning!" I smiled and tugged at the buttons on my coat.

Will scrambled out of his seat and insisted on helping me. He slid the wool garment off my shoulders and hung it on the coat hook at the end of the booth.

Iris appeared, glaring at me with a sullen expression as she poured my coffee.

Will and I sat down, smiling at each other.

"You're early—"

"I tried to get here sooner—"

We laughed.

"You go—"

"Your turn—"

We laughed again.

He held up his hand to silence me. "Ladies first. *Go.*"

"I wish I could get here earlier," I said and rested my chin on the heel of my hand. "I'd like to have breakfast with you, but a half-hour is rushing things."

"Why is that? Doesn't the Harvmobile operate any earlier?"

I laughed again. "It's not that. Francie is still attending her old school and she starts her first class at the same time I'm due to the office. So that's why I can't get here more than a couple of minutes before seven-thirty." I sighed. "I wish I knew how to drive."

"You do?" He looked genuinely surprised. "Why do you need to drive a car when you can afford a chauffeur to take you wherever you want to go?"

"Because I want the freedom of being able to drive myself!" I stared at him, frustrated. Why did men always assume I needed their help? Was it because I only stood five feet, two inches tall, or did the problem exist simply because I was a woman? "Besides, I own a Ford dealership. I should know how to drive my own vehicles, shouldn't I?"

He didn't say anything at first and I wondered if my declaration had sounded arrogant. "I agree," he said suddenly. "You should learn to drive if that's what you want to do." He held up his coffee cup in a salute. "Look out world. Here comes Charlotte LeDoux."

*   *   *

Later that day, I was in the nursery with Julien when Lillian, my maid, appeared at the door. The tall, willowy woman wore her light brown hair short and parted on the side with soft waves. She gave me a pleasant smile. "You have a visitor, My Lady," she said in a soft, feminine voice.

Really? My first visitor!

I'd given the security guard a pre-approved list of names of people they could allow to enter the grounds without checking with my staff first, so it had to be someone I knew.

Julien's nanny, Gretchen, had left the room temporarily to dispose of a soiled diaper and I didn't want to wait for her to return so I picked up my son and carried him downstairs with me. As I descended the wide staircase, I found Will standing in the cavernous hall clutching his hat in his hand, awaiting my arrival. He wore a navy, double-breasted pinstripe suit and a white shirt with a matching navy tie. The bold, woodsy scent of his cologne wafted my way, causing my heart to tap a little dance. He beamed when he saw me. "Are you ready?"

I didn't understand what he meant. "For what?"

"You said you wanted to learn to drive. Or have you changed your mind since breakfast?"

"Absolutely not!" Julien began to wiggle in my arms and I shifted him to my hip. "I didn't realize you thought I was asking you to teach me."

"No matter." He walked toward me. "I'm here so let's go."

I don't know why, but I suddenly began to panic. "Now? But...I...I..."

"But what?" His joviality turned to disappointment. He stared at Julien. "Don't you have someone to mind the baby? What about your sister?"

"Well, of course, I do. Francie's at the library returning books, but Gretchen is—"

Will silenced me by setting his hat on the hall table and pulling Julien from my arms. "So, this is your little guy. He sure looks like his daddy." He ruffled Julien's fine, golden hair. "Hello there!" Julien stared up at Will, wide-eyed, but he didn't cry.

Lillian came down the stairs and approached us, curiously staring at Will holding my child. As soon as she reached us, Will handed the baby to her. "Here you go." He turned to me. "I'll get your coat."

"I'll be back later," I said to Lillian. "Tell Gretchen to put Julien to bed without me."

I followed Will to the closet and pulled out a light jacket. The temperature today had reached sixty degrees and there wasn't a cloud in the sky, but evenings were usually cool. He helped me put it on and opened the door for me. "After you."

We left through the main entrance, into the carriage porch where Will had parked his late-model Ford. The convertible top was down on the black vehicle and as I came down the steps, I stared at the Model T in fear. Talking about learning to drive and actually *getting behind the wheel* was as different as night and day. I had a mind to turn around and run right back into the house, but Will must have sensed my reluctance and kept a firm grip on my arm.

"All right then," he said in a serious tone and opened the door on the passenger side. "We're going to go over the basic information first." He reached out and pulled up the top of the wide bench seat, revealing a long and square metal tank beneath it. "This is the gas tank. The first thing you do, before you start the car, is to check the gas level with your gauge." He placed his hand on the tank, his face etched in a deep frown. "You *never* want to run out of gas and end up stranded somewhere." He unscrewed the cap and picked up a long wooden measuring stick. "You use this." He stuck the stick into the tank and pulled it out. "See the mark here?" He pointed to where the gas had wet the stick. "Looks like we've got about five gallons. That'll take you about a hundred miles."

Okay, I thought, gaining confidence. *This isn't going to be as bad as it first seemed.*

He replaced the cap, lowered the seat to its original position, and took me around to the front of the car. For the next five minutes, we went over how to start a cold engine, but since the car had recently been driven, we didn't need to go through the physical exercise of cranking it. The car would perform a "hot" start.

Will opened the driver's side door. "Get in. You're going to start it up."

I hopped into the driver's seat excited to get going at last. *What's so hard about this? All I have to do is turn the key.*

Will got into the passenger side. "Okay." He pointed to three pedals on the floor. "From right to left, you've got the brake, the middle one is the reverse pedal and the last one is the clutch. It works with the hand brake lever, that tall stick on your left."

Wha—what? I let out a deep breath. *Okay*... I stored those facts in my head, hoping it would all become clearer once we got started. "How do you make the car...go?"

Will pointed to two levers on the steering column. "The one on the right is the throttle. It controls the automobile's speed. The one on the left is the spark advance to adjust the timing of the engine. Make sure the spark advance lever is all the way forward but pull slightly on the throttle. Good, now turn the key."

I did as he instructed and nothing happened. I turned my head sideways and stared at him. "What went wrong?"

"You have to step on the starter. It's that square on the floor behind the pedals."

"Oh, okay," I said and looked down, feeling frustrated. *Turn this, adjust that, now step on the floor—how am I ever going to remember all of these instructions the next time I do this?*

I pushed on the large rubber square with my foot and the car started. I began to laugh with excitement. I did it! I started the car!

Will scooted close to me and slid his long arm behind me across the back of the seat. The unique aroma of his cologne filled my nostrils. *Oh, my goodness...*

"Now," he said in my ear, "pull the spark advance lever down to adjust the timing."

I slowly pulled on the left lever and the engine began running faster. The butterflies in my stomach kept pace with the engine.

Will turned the ignition key to the right to "Magneto" to save on the batteries. "Put your foot on the clutch and pull the hand brake forward halfway."

I did what he told me to do and the car lurched forward. I hadn't expected it to actually *move*! Screaming in panic, I moved my foot to the brake pedal but the car didn't stop.

It went in reverse.

"Will!"

"You're fine," Will said calmly into my ear as he moved his foot to the brake and stopped the car. "Get your foot off the reverse pedal and go back to the clutch." He cupped his arm around my shoulders as I obeyed and the car went forward again. "We're off!"

My fingers tightened on the steering wheel with a death grip as the car slowly rolled down the driveway. My nerves were so sharply on edge my clothes were drenched in sweat under my jacket. Hal, one of my nighttime security guards, had already opened the gates for us and stood outside the guard shack with a big smile on his face, waving as we rolled on by. Going through the gates, I didn't dare look anywhere but straight ahead for fear the car would veer to one side and crash. I was so short I could barely see over the steering wheel. Cars were definitely made for men only! We came to the end of the driveway and I correctly stepped on the brake.

From the corner of my eye, I saw Will grinning. "See? That wasn't so bad, was it?"

Maybe not, but I was so afraid of colliding with other cars on the road, I felt like throwing up.

I turned my head to tell him I didn't know if I could go on and realized that if he tipped his head slightly, his lips would be touching mine. At any other time, the prospect would have thrilled me to my toes, but kissing was the last thing on my mind right now. I just wanted to get through this session with the car in one piece!

He pointed toward Summit Avenue. "Okay, now let's get out on the road. Turn left."

I stared at the street, gripped with a new level of fear. "You—you mean, drive in traffic?"

"Come on, it's the only way you're going to learn." When I swallowed hard, he whispered in my ear, "Don't worry, darling. You're doing fine."

Did he just call me darling?

If we were at home, I would have reacted differently, but I was sitting behind the wheel of a mechanical monster and about to pull out into the flow of traffic so I couldn't concentrate on anything else. After checking—three times—to make sure the road was clear, I slowly turned the vehicle onto Summit Avenue.

Will adjusted the throttle and the car went faster.

Oh, dear Lord!

My hands had a stranglehold on the steering wheel.

After a couple of blocks, something amazing happened; my stomach stopped churning and the rigidness in my shoulders began to relax. The early evening air blew in my face, easing my tension and refreshing me. We kept going until we came upon a red stoplight. I put my foot on the brake, bringing the car to a complete stop. "This is turning out to be fun!"

I laughed and turned my head to see why Will didn't have anything to say. He stared deeply into my eyes and before I realized what was on his mind, he kissed me. A light, soft kiss that was over as quickly as it started. Even so, I sat frozen, taking in the moment as my stomach fluttered with fresh butterflies, but this time for an utterly fascinating reason—I wanted more. I slipped my arms around his neck and began to kiss him back.

The people behind us voiced their protest with loud honks. The light had turned green.

Laughing, we separated and I adjusted the throttle to start the car moving again, but my mind had slipped into high gear. The minty taste of his lips surprised me and I craved more. I silently held out my hand and kept it extended until he realized what I wanted. He dropped a Pep-O-Mint Life Saver into my palm and I popped it into my mouth. Next time—and there would absolutely be one—I wanted him to have the same great-tasting kiss that I'd experienced!

We drove around for another hour until we spotted one of my soda shops. We stopped for an ice cream sundae and a short break then got back on the road again. By the time I pulled into the circular drive in front of my house, the sun had long set. Although the light had been left on inside the carriage porch, Will instructed me to pull past it and park in a dark spot. I knew why…

As soon as I shut off the car, he pulled me into his arms and kissed me in a deep, passionate kiss. I slid my arms around his neck and leaned into his broad chest, caught up in the intensity of the moment.

"I've wanted to do this ever since the night I met up with you at the Tansy Club," he murmured huskily. The rhythm of his heartbeat marched in sync with mine as we held each other close.

"All I wanted that night was to go home. I wasn't enjoying myself at all," I replied softly. "That is until I met up with you. I had more fun sitting with you at the diner than I'd had in a long time."

He pulled back. "That uproar at the Tansy Club was hardly what I'd call a fun night. I barely got you out of there before the place came apart at the seams."

I sighed. "It wasn't my fault that Benny and Leonard wouldn't back down. I've never had two men fight over me before."

He chuckled. "That's because you used to be married to someone who'd snuff a guy out if he looked twice at you." He kissed me again, holding me like he didn't want to let me go. "Now that you're one of the most sought-after women in town, I'm sure it won't be the last time it happens."

"Will! You slay me!" I laughed, splaying my palms against his chest. "I'm not one of the most sought-after females in town. I only leave my house to go to the office and when I do, it's not as though I go around looking for trouble. On the contrary. It seems to always find me."

"You just don't know, do you?"

I pulled back, totally baffled. "Know what?"

He stroked his thumb across my cheek. "The effect you have on men."

What? I scoffed to hide my embarrassment. "What are you talking about?"

He lifted his hand and slid a lock of hair behind my ear. "A pretty little woman with a lot of spunk—men find it irresistible."

I went completely still, absorbing that information. So, men found me attractive because I was short, stubborn, and persistent? I hoped Will was including himself in that amusing explanation. "The only man I want to have an effect on is *you*."

He paused for a moment as if weighing his response. "Then have dinner with me."

This time I wasn't letting the opportunity slip by. "When?"

"Friday night," he said eagerly. "I'll take you anywhere you want to go."

A thought crossed my mind. "How would you like to come here for dinner? Francie is going to an overnight birthday party and I know someone who'll watch the baby for me. We'll have the house to ourselves. I'll cook something special."

He placed his hand under my chin and tilted my head back so he could look deeply into my eyes. The light from the carriage porch illuminated the five-o-clock shadow darkening his jaw. "Would you mind having a helper? I can't guarantee how much help I'll be, but I'd love to give it a try."

"It's a date, Mr. Van Elsberg. No need to bring a bottle of hooch. I've got a wine cellar filled with any variety your heart desires."

His eyes shone in the silvery light. "I'll be there."

Chapter Seven

The next afternoon, I stood on the front steps of my house as the brothers' shiny black Rolls Royce—the "Harvmobile" as Will called it—glided to a stop inside the carriage porch. Harv's paid goons were riding shotgun in the car behind them.

The chauffeur got out of the Rolls and opened the door for me. I slid in and found Harv waiting for me with a glass of wine. I thanked him and took a sip. Hmmm…Bordeaux; Harv's passion of late. "Is Marv on his way to Seattle?" His train was scheduled to leave this morning.

Harv nodded as he poured himself a fresh glass of wine. I could see he wasn't in a particularly good mood and I wondered why. "Have you uncovered yet who this mystery person is that wants to buy La Coquette?"

"No," he said, sounding irritated. "When I pressed the attorney representing him, the only answer I could get was that we'd find out at the appointment."

Ah-ah. I snorted. "Sounds like a man of ill repute."

Harv grunted. "I don't care if he's the King of England. You're the seller and the price must be satisfactory to you or there is no deal."

"That's *if* I decide to sell it." I sat back and stared out the window.

"At this point, I don't know what I want to do with the place. It's a beautiful building and it used to be Gus' pride and joy." I sighed. "I don't know if I'm ready to part with it yet."

We drank our wine in silence for the rest of the journey. When the car pulled into the front of the brick building, I didn't see any other cars in the parking lot and wondered if the potential buyer had changed his mind.

I stared out the window and the horror of my last night in this place came flooding back in a swift flash. It should have been the best night of my life, but instead, it ended in tragedy.

I had planned to give Gus the wonderful news that after nine years of heartbreaking miscarriages, I was finally going to have a baby—but I never got the chance. My happiness had been cruelly derailed when I found him locked in his office with another woman. Before I could get him alone to have it out with him, Federal Agents stormed the building. Amid the ensuing chaos, Gus forced me to leave with his right-hand man, Albert, claiming I'd be safer with him. But when an agent's gunshot took Albert's life, I decided to disappear and let Gus think I'd died as well. I couldn't bring myself to raise a child in my husband's world of violence, betrayal, and uncertainty.

The car stopped at the front door. It had been eleven months since that fateful night, but seeing the place again overwhelmed me with anxiety, as though it had only happened yesterday. Reluctantly, I got out of the car and followed Harv into the building. From the lobby, I peered into the ballroom and as I got a glimpse of the widespread destruction, my breath quickened. The place had been overflowing with patrons the night the Feds raided the establishment. When the crowd panicked and stormed the exits, they'd obliterated everything in their way.

Harv and I walked past the coatroom and entered the enormous ballroom. Tables and chairs were strewn across the cavernous room, many smashed into pieces. Dishes, silverware, and broken glass crunched under my feet. I gazed at the wide stage where a twelve-piece orchestra once played and where every weekend our twenty-five-member dance team would perform a new show. Now, only overturned chairs and rusting music stands occupied the space. Yellowed pieces of sheet music and grime covered the wooden floor. Two stories up, the crystal chandeliers, once sparkling and elegant, hung lifeless and dull under a thick layer of dust.

It was so cold where we stood, I could see my breath. Dampness chilled me to the bone. I heard something scurry behind me and turned to see a large raccoon disappear under a pile of rubble. My memories of the beauty of this place had been completely overridden by this new reality. It was as if La Coquette had never existed.

"Ah, there you are."

Harv and I spun around to find Leonard Murtagh and his attorney, Alvin Brady standing in the doorway in their dark, hand-tailored suits, and their black fedoras angled low over their brows. Alvin was of medium height with salt and pepper hair. Leonard looked the same as he did at the Tansy Club—short, dark hair combed back, gunmetal-blue eyes, and a dimpled chin. His sharp gaze scanned my body with lightning speed the moment he saw me. I moved closer to Harv and stared right back.

Of all the nerve...

Leonard Murtagh had certainly sought to elevate himself in the crime world since his days as Gus' former bodyguard and driver. Criminals were no longer part of my peer group, especially a man who reputedly fancied himself becoming the next Gus LeDoux—the king of bootleggers. I had no time for this bum.

"Gentlemen," Harv said crisply but didn't extend his hand to shake with either man. "Shall we get started?" He made a sweeping gesture with his arm. "The building is for sale *as is*. Would you care to look around before we discuss the price?"

Leonard and his attorney exchanged whispers.

"Yes," Alvin said directly to Harv, ignoring me as though I had no more importance in this deal than a strip of the faded wallpaper. "We'll start at the lower level with the gambling rooms and work our way upward."

Harv turned to me. "You don't need to go down there, honey. It's dark and musty. You wait here. I'll take care of this."

I turned my back at an angle so Leonard couldn't see my response. "Actually, there is something else I want to look at so I'll do that while you're showing them around."

"All right, but be careful." He shoved a broken chair out of his way with his foot. "Watch your step when you're looking around. This place is full of debris. I wouldn't want you to fall and hurt yourself."

I waited until the men were out of sight before I headed for the stairway and bolted upstairs. It was a short walk down the hallway to Gus' office, but when I arrived, the door was shut. I tried the handle. It was also locked.

That's odd. Gus couldn't have been in much of a hurry to get away if he'd taken the time to lock the door behind him…

But that didn't make sense. He didn't have more than a minute or two that night to escape before the Feds invaded the building. Locking the door would have been the last thing on his mind. Besides, if he *would* have locked the door, the Feds would have smashed in.

I walked to the end of the hallway and pulled up the corner of the carpet behind a dead palm tree in a dark red and gold oriental urn. To my relief, the key was still there. I grabbed it and unlocked the door. I wrinkled my nose at the musty air and the dust that had settled on everything.

The Federal agents who had raided this room must have been looking for key evidence to charge Gus for his crimes. All of the desk drawers had been emptied onto the floor and all of the books in the bookcases had been pulled off. Unfortunately for the Feds, Gus never kept any of his books or anything else incriminating in this office. I didn't have a clue as to where he kept his accounting ledgers, but it didn't matter anymore.

I stepped over the rubble as I walked around the room, searching for some clue to tell me what had happened here on that day nearly a year ago. I searched under the furniture, looked behind the pictures on the wall, and even tried to pull up the carpet, but it wouldn't budge.

Standing in the middle of the room, I stared long and hard at the scene, saddened by the destruction. Gus was organized to a fault and this place had been turned into a depressing mess. On the floor, next to my foot, I saw a small wooden pheasant figurine. Hand-carved and hand-painted, it had been one of Gus' favorite items because his younger brother had made it for him in school. It had faded considerably.

Dismayed, I picked it up and walked over to the bookcase to put it back in the spot on the shelf it used to occupy. That's when I saw it. A fine crack between two of the bookcases on the wall. It was caused because they were slightly uneven—the middle one and the one on the right. I'd never noticed it before but I knew that the old carpenter who'd built them would never have been guilty of such flawed work. Time and humidity must have forced the bookcases to shift. I wondered if something had fallen or been shoved behind it. I grabbed the shelf and pulled on it, fully expecting it to give way, but it didn't. Instead, the entire bookcase began to move forward.

Shocked and curious at the same time, I gingerly kept pulling. I was worried I might find myself on my derriere on the floor with an empty bookcase on top of me, but after a few tugs, the structure slid straight out on concealed rollers. I peeked behind it and gasped. In the wall, I found an opening about five feet high that revealed a narrow wooden staircase. My heart began to pound.

I hurried over to the office door and engaged the deadbolt lock. I didn't want anyone to find me in here, or worse yet, to find the secret I'd just discovered. Going back to the opening, I looked up the staircase and realized it led to an area with plenty of light. Curious, I kept going. The wooden treads creaked under my feet as I slowly mounted the steep stairs, advancing upward until I came into a narrow, roughly-hewn room with a slanted ceiling at the very top of the building. On both ends of the room was a square, slatted vent camouflaging a cottage window on the inside.

The room was sparsely furnished with a couple of chairs, a small table, candles, and several bedrolls. In one corner I found an empty water jug and a small box containing a discarded biscuit tin and packages of crackers. The floor was covered with a thick rug to muffle footsteps.

So, this was how Gus managed to elude the Feds. He held out here until everyone had left the building and then slipped away.

There were other boxes and a suitcase to inspect, but a feeling of urgency washed over me. No way did I want anyone to discover this room! I hurried back down the steep, narrow stairway and when I reached the bottom tread, I saw how the bookcase could be bolted to the stairwell from the inside, making a tight seal over the opening. I slipped through the opening again and pushed the bookcase back to its original position. With the key in my pocket, I shut the door again and started to make my way back to the ballroom to wait for the men. I didn't get far.

Leonard bolted up the stairs and met me in the hallway. He looked surprised to find me there and just as curious. "What are you doing up here?" He stopped in front of me, moving so close I had a mind to back up a step, but I didn't want him to know he made me nervous.

With a defiant lift of my chin, I stared up at him. "I haven't seen this place since it was raided. I wanted to know what happened to it. What do you think I was doing up here?"

He gave me an amused look. "Maybe you were hunting around,

looking for a stash of money or guns."

I responded with an incredulous laugh at that assertion. "If I thought Gus had stored either one of those items in this place, do you think I would have waited this long to search for it?" I purposely sounded annoyed, letting him know I found him tedious at best. I started to walk past him. "I need to find Harv."

"Wait." He clasped his fingers around my arm and stopped me. "You and me need to have a serious talk about the future of this place."

I turned my head. "We can talk downstairs."

"No," he snapped, "I don't want that old man gettin' in the way. This deal is between us."

I shook his hand off my arm. "If you plan to make an offer on this building, it must go through Harv."

"I've got a better idea," he said, changing his tone. "How about the two of us reopening this joint together? You handle the staff and the entertainment like you did before. I'll run the gambling operation and furnish the liquor."

I nearly swallowed my tongue. "You can't be serious."

"Listen, doll, this place was a gold mine before it was closed down. It was even more classy than the Tansy Club and we could easily turn it into a moneymaker again. You could double your fortune if you revived it, but you can't do it alone." He gave me a sly grin. "That's where I come in. You'd need a partner, someone to handle the business end of things. I got a buddy with good connections at City Hall who'd like a piece of the action, too."

By the *business end*, I knew exactly what he meant—handling the money. His words made me so mad I wondered if he could see steam rolling off me. "I'm nobody's *doll*, Leonard, and if I ever decide to reopen La Coquette, I won't need *you* or some chump who's good at bribing officials to handle my business affairs. I'm fully capable of operating this place myself."

His eyes narrowed. "You wouldn't last a month without Katzenbaum riding shotgun over everything you do, Charlotte." He grabbed me by the chin, gripping my jaw so tightly it hurt. "I could have him bumped off before dinner and then who would protect you, eh, little lady?"

I wrenched my chin from his grasp and shoved him away. "Don't threaten me, Murtagh. You're not the only one who knows how to shoot a gun."

"Yeah, like that slug you put in your old man with his own piece?" His lips curved into a smug smile.

I stood frozen with shock. How did he know about that? He wasn't there! My heart began to hammer. The room started to spin, but my feet responded to the urgency to get away as I began backing toward the stairway. "I'll give this place to charity before I'll go into business with *you*. This appointment is over. Get out and don't come back!"

I clung to the banister as I ran down the stairway, righting myself when I nearly stumbled on the bottom stair. I found Harv and Alvin Brady having a heated discussion in the ballroom. "I know what's going on," I said in response to Harv's concerned look as I headed straight for the front door, "and these two are just wasting my time because I'm not falling for it. I'll wait for you in the car."

Harv rounded up Leonard and Alvin Brady and the three of them followed me out. I didn't say anything until Harv and I were on our way to the office. I rarely used liquor to soothe my nerves, but I'd poured myself a glass of wine the moment I'd crawled into the car and I already needed a refill. "I told Leonard I'd give the building to charity before I'd go into business with him." Holding out my glass for more wine, I took a deep breath. "I want nothing more to do with that life."

The city flew by as I stared out the window and sipped my wine. How did Leonard know I'd shot Gus with his own gun?

74

He'd betrayed Gus somehow. Deep in my heart, I sensed it. I didn't know what he'd done, but I intended to find out. In the meantime, I wondered if he'd told anyone else what he knew about me and whether he could actually prove it.

I desperately needed to talk to Will.

*   *   *

I didn't expect Will to show up for coffee the next morning. He'd gone undercover for several days to gather information on a case. I wouldn't see him until Friday night, but it gave me time to plan out every morsel of our dinner.

Of all the meals I'd cooked for Will when I worked as his housekeeper and cook, beef dishes were the ones he'd enjoyed most. I spoke with my cook and went through her recipe book to find the perfect entree to make for our special dinner. At the same time, she recommended a couple of other dishes to round out the meal.

I left the office early on Thursday and when I arrived home, I spent some time with Julien then changed into a wool skirt and sweater to go to the market. My Ford dealership on West Seventh Street had delivered my new black Roadster, a smart-looking, two-door vehicle with a soft top and I couldn't wait to take it for a drive. Chet, the daytime security guard on duty, walked over to the car to watch me start it up—and eagerly offered to lend a hand if I experienced any difficulty. With some helpful advice from Chet, I went through the procedure, and my "Tin Lizzie," as Will called it, started up without any difficulty.

Francie asked me for a ride to the library on my way, so I dropped her off first. She'd taken quite an interest in reading lately and I wondered if one of her teachers had encouraged her to explore the world of classic fiction. It also surprised me because lately, she'd shown less interest in school than ever and had become difficult to get out of bed every morning.

Of course, now that I had learned to drive, *she* wanted to learn too.

She couldn't wait for the new car to be delivered so her friends at the library could see us roll up to the building in the roadster.

"I'll pick you up at six-thirty," I said as I pulled up to the library and stepped on the brake. "Don't dawdle. The staff will get worried if we're not home for dinner by seven o'clock sharp, so we have to be on our way immediately."

Francie opened the door on her side of the car and hopped out. "When are you going to teach me to drive?"

When your grades improve and you're three years older…

I kept that comment to myself for now. The last thing I needed this weekend was to start an ongoing argument with my sister. As it was, we argued constantly over her taking my cosmetics, clothing, shoes, and jewelry without my permission. She had no shortage of nice things, but did that stop her from helping herself to everything I owned? Sigh…

"We'll talk about it later. I've got to get going."

I went to the market and found everything on my list in the time I had allotted. I could have simply had my cook call the store and order the groceries, but I wanted to select the ingredients for the dinner myself.

I drove into the library parking lot at twenty-five minutes after six and left the car running as I walked up to the building. Pulling open the front door, I peered inside, hoping to see Francie checking out her new library books. To my dismay, she wasn't in the main area.

Impatient to get going, I quickly walked through the library and peered down the aisles of bookcases, hoping to find her busily reading something, but she was nowhere to be found. I checked the ladies' room and found it empty.

An elderly lady in a long, traditional black dress with a high neck and long sleeves approached me. "May I help you?"

"I'm looking for my sister, Francie. She has short blonde hair and she's wearing a blue skirt and blouse."

The woman's expression changed from politeness to severe disapproval as she nodded and pointed toward the back door. "Try looking out there."

I rushed to the back door and pulled it open. Francie sat on a picnic table under a large budding crabapple tree—with Elliott Cohn—and they weren't discussing their favorite books. They were locked in a kiss so ardent it made my heart sink. My sister was too young to get romantically involved with a young man—and especially that one!

I folded my arms and cleared my throat. They both saw me at the same time.

Elliott's face took on a peeved expression.

Francie scowled.

"*Well*, I see why you're so interested in coming to the library," I snapped. "We're leaving, Francie. Now!"

Francie said goodbye to Elliott and followed me, sulking like a child. In the parking lot, she got into the car and slammed the door. "You're not Mamma. You have no right to tell me what to do!"

"I promised her I'd watch over you and that's what I'm doing!"

Gripping the steering wheel tight enough to strangle it, I had all I could do to keep from driving straight over to Leon Goldman's home and cussing him out about the nephew he was supposed to be supervising. It would have to wait until after tomorrow, but I definitely planned to pay a visit to Leon, and when I'd finished with him, Elliott Cohn would be a distant memory.

Chapter Eight

"Your guest has arrived, My Lady."

Gerard stood in the doorway of the kitchen, down in the lower level, where I stood at the center island going over my ingredients list. I wanted to make sure I had everything to make dinner tonight with Will.

"Thank you, Gerard." I pulled off my apron and threw it on the counter. "I'll take it from here."

The older, heavyset man stared at my preparations, bewildered at my presence in the servants' domain. "Are you sure you won't be needing assistance with preparing and serving your meal?"

"I'll be fine." I stopped and patted him on the shoulder on my way out of the kitchen. "And I absolutely want you to take the rest of the night off. Remind all of the staff they're off, too."

I had arranged for Mrs. Olson, a sweet, elderly woman who lived across the alley from Mamma's former house to take Julien for the evening. Mrs. Olson had occasionally watched Julien for me back when Mamma was alive. I trusted her completely.

"Very good." Gerard bowed. "The dining room has been set for your dinner. I'll see you at breakfast."

"Thank you. Have a good night off."

He bowed again, looking bewildered at my excitement over cooking my own meal as I breezed past him and ran upstairs.

I found Will waiting for me in the airy, spacious reception hall. He wore a dark brown pinstripe suit and a white shirt. "Will! Are you ready to learn how to cook?"

"Absolutely." He smiled and held out a small package wrapped in white tissue paper. "For you."

"Thank you," I said and proceeded to tear off the wrapping. When I saw what he'd given me, I squealed with delight. "Oh, my gosh!"

He looked mystified at my glee. "You really like it? I'm afraid it's not glamorous, like flowers or candy."

"Minnie's cookbook? Of course, I like it! I love it!" Minnie was deceased now, but she had been his family's cook for many years. I'd discovered her cookbook in a kitchen drawer back when I worked as Will's cook and housekeeper and had used it to prepare many of his meals. I curled my arm around his. "Come along. We've got a meal to fix."

I took him down to the kitchen and helped him out of his suit coat then proceeded to tie a chef's apron around him. He took it all in stride, laughing at my insistence that he needed to look like a proper chef. In truth, I didn't want him to get food stains on his starched white shirt.

Will noticed four bottles of wine sitting on the counter along with a wine key. He picked up the closest one, examining it. "What's this, two for you and two for me?"

I laughed. "I didn't know what kind you prefer, so I picked out an assortment. If you don't like any of those, I'll take you down to the wine cellar and you can choose something else."

"These are fine." Will selected a bottle of chardonnay. "Let's give this one a try." He opened it and filled two glasses. We clinked our glasses together in a toast to a great meal and took our first sip. The oaky, buttery liquid slid over my tongue with a hint of sweetness. Hmmm…I took another one.

Time to get to work… I set down my glass and pulled two containers from the walk-in ice room, one filled with round steak, the other with salt pork. My cook had already ground the beef for us and sliced the pork so all we had to do was add the ingredients and bake it. I informed Will he was the lead cook for this dish and placed the recipe on the counter for him.

"How many people are we feeding?" Will asked as he looked at the recipe and began to add the ingredients into a huge bowl. Adeline—or "Cook," as she called herself—had measured everything into small containers so all he had to do was find the right ones and add them to the meat.

I sipped more wine. "Just the two of us. It's a big recipe, I know, but the staff can have the leftovers. I gave them the night off and Francie's at an overnight birthday party for one of her girlfriends."

Will looked up. "So, we're all alone in this big house?"

I nodded and absently sipped more wine. "No babies crying, no servants underfoot. We can simply enjoy our dinner."

He refilled our glasses. "How is Francie getting along without her mother?"

"Well…" I said as I leaned against the counter, "she's coping with it, but other issues are becoming more problematic by the day."

"I assume this has something to do with Goldman's nephew." He picked up a long-handled wooden spoon and began to stir the ingredients into the beef.

"You assumed right." I proceeded to tell him about the library incident as I buttered the loaf pan, adding that I'd made sure to verify Francie's attendance at the birthday party to avoid the possibility of an all-night rendezvous with young Mr. Cohn.

"Leon needs to be informed." Will dumped the beef into the loaf pan and smoothed the top with his spoon. "I'll pay him a visit and let him know how you feel if you'd like."

"Thanks for the offer, but I'd like to talk to him myself," I said and pressed slices of salt pork across the top of the beef. "I want him to understand it's personal."

I set the wind-up timer and then opened the oven door for Will. He slid the beef dish into it. As soon as I closed the door and straightened up, he took me into his arms. "Don't worry. Everything will work out," he said as he rested his cheek on the top of my head. "Francie is just going through normal issues for a girl her age. She'll eventually straighten out."

I sighed as I melted against his broad chest. "I hope you're right." His strong, but tender grip gave me a much-needed feeling of comfort and safety. I could handle my own problems, but sometimes it felt good to know I had someone to talk to when I needed advice or simply desired a sympathetic ear.

He released me and helped himself to more wine. I handed him a paring knife. "Next order of business is to peel potatoes."

I spread out a sheet of newspaper and grabbed a bowl of raw potatoes from the counter. We drank wine while we peeled them for a side dish called Delmonico Potatoes. Once the potatoes were sliced, we placed them in a baking dish with pre-prepared white sauce that Cook had made ahead of time for us, salt, pepper, and butter. We covered the mixture with cracker crumbs and cheese and slipped the dish into the oven next to the beef.

Will refilled our glasses with the last of the white wine. "What's next, Betty Crocker?"

I laughed and threw a hand towel at him, but he ducked and the towel narrowly missed my wine glass. "We're making shrimp salad." I handed him a can of shrimp to open and drain while I rinsed the lettuce.

81

I sliced up the celery and lemon for garnish. Together, we mixed the salad ingredients with mayonnaise and scooped it onto lettuce leaves arranged on small plates. We added the lemon garnish and set them in the ice room to stay cool.

Our wine consumption was beginning to slow us down, but I didn't care. For our dessert, we tried to whip the cream and kept sloshing it over the side of the bowl. Our clumsiness made us laugh as we continually wiped spills off the counter. Eventually, we did get it whipped to the right consistency and added pineapple, marshmallow pieces, chopped walnuts, and coconut then spooned it into several small dishes. It was a good thing I'd taken the precaution to have everything pre-measured beforehand or this meal would have been a disaster. I tried to open a jar of maraschino cherries, but it slipped from my hands and nearly spun off the counter before Will caught it. He opened the jar and pulled out a cherry, dropping it in my wine glass.

"Hey," I protested with a giggle, "that's a topping for the dessert."

Will popped a couple of cherries into his mouth. "How's this for dessert," he said in a husky voice and gave me a cherry-flavored kiss. I'd had so much wine I had to grip his shoulders to stand up.

Thankfully, the timer went off, cutting short our session of horsing around. We opened the oven and checked our beef. The meat dish was done to perfection and the potatoes were baked to a golden brown.

"Okay, let's eat!" I walked over to the dumbwaiter and opened the door. "Everything goes in here, cold food in the first shipment then hot food in the next one." I stumbled to the doorway. "You fill the dumbwaiter and send it up. I'll go upstairs and take everything out."

By the time I arrived upstairs, the cold food was already waiting for me. I set it on a cart and rolled the cart into the dining room to set it on the sideboard. Will sent up the second round and ran upstairs—carrying an opened bottle of red wine—before I had the chance to empty the service lift. He rolled the cart into the dining room with the hot food and set it on the sideboard.

"We're missing the serving spoons!" I looked around, realizing we'd forgotten to bring a few from the kitchen.

Will looked at me, confused. "Do you want me to go back to the kitchen and look for some?"

I laughed. "No need. We'll just get them from the silver vault." I walked over to the wall. Hidden in the elaborately carved wainscoting was a small metal medallion the size of a button. I pressed on it and the panel opened to a tall, but narrow vault, like the one in the den. I spun the combination on the dial and the vault opened. Inside the narrow closet filled with silver service pieces, I found the spoons and grabbed a half-dozen then closed the vault.

We filled our plates, pushed our chairs together, and sat down to eat.

"This is what I miss the most about when you lived with me," Will said as he dug into his beef. "You're the best cook in the world, Char." He looked up. "Even better than Minnie."

"Aw-w-w…" I said, truly flattered. To have a man say that he loved my culinary talent more than his own family's cook was a once-in-a-lifetime compliment.

"You're so good to me." He held up his fork, covered with a morsel of beef, to feed me. I ate the food and tried to think of the right words to say in return, but my mind was getting more muddled by the minute.

He filled our wine glasses again and raised his glass to make a toast. "To your fantastic cooking, Char. It's always good, but my favorite is your baked ribs. They're the best!" We clinked our glasses together and drained them. Then I remembered something…

I gasped.

"What's the matter?" Will frowned. "Did you burn your tongue?"

I shook my head. "I just thought of…something. Leonard…"

The tone of my voice must have alarmed him. Will set down his fork, his eyes narrowed. "What about Leonard?" Even through my wine-induced haze, I could tell he'd taken my comment with grave seriousness.

"He knows…" I said fearfully. "I don't know how he found out, but he knows I killed Gus. He taunted me with it the other day when he showed up to pitch that ridiculous offer to co-manage La Coquette. I don't know what he has planned, but it's apparent he's going to use it against me." My eyes filled with tears. "How? How would he know? You and I were the only ones in that alley when it happened."

Overwhelmed, I jumped out of my chair and ran from the room.

Will caught up to me at the stairway and surrounded me with his arms. "Listen to me," he said in a commanding voice, trying to calm my hysteria. "He's not going to blackmail you to get his hands on La Coquette, understand? I don't care what he thinks he knows, he's a crook whose word means nothing." He lifted my face to look into my eyes. "If it comes down to your word against his, remember, I was there, too. My story is and always will be that Gus got into a shootout with an agent and they killed each other." His fervent gaze bored into mine. "I'll never allow anyone to hurt you, Char." He tightened his grip on me. "You mean everything to me."

"Oh, Will…" I whispered, stunned. It all made sense to me now. The way he always looked into my eyes when we talked. The soft tone in his voice when we spoke. The little things he did to tease me and make me laugh. The way he'd suddenly kissed me that day he was teaching me to drive. He'd been demonstrating his feelings for me more and more each day. Deep in my heart, I'd always cared for him, too—but with so much going on in my life I'd blocked it out, afraid to get distracted from all the balls I needed to keep suspended in the air. All that had passed now. There was nothing to hold me back.

"My life has been crazy. I'm glad you never gave up on me." I rested my palms on his chest, mesmerized by the spellbinding passion in his eyes. "I don't want anything to separate us ever again."

His fingers deftly traced the length of my bare arm and slipped the thin strap of my dress off my shoulder. He began to kiss a trail from my shoulder to my neck, sending tremors through me. Tipping my head back, I closed my eyes, swept up in the heat of the moment. In the back of my mind, I knew where this would lead, but my heart didn't want him to stop...

*   *   *

The next morning, I awoke in my bed—alone. Sometime during the night, Will had left but I'd had so much to drink that my memory of the entire evening was mostly a blur. I *did* remember the way he had burned kisses into my bare neck—

The thought startled me, but at the same time, it hurt so much to process anything in my mind I could barely think. My head pounded so hard it felt like it could explode at any minute. *Ugh.* We should have never consumed that second bottle of wine.

I swear I'll never touch another glass of wine as long as I live!

I sat up to press the call button for my morning coffee but found myself overcome with dizziness and immediately collapsed back on the bed.

Within a couple of minutes, Lillian walked into my room with a breakfast tray. "Good morning, My Lady." She, and the rest of the staff, addressed me in the same manner as Gerard. She set down the tray and opened the drapes, filling the room with bright sunlight as I squinted and struggled to sit up. "Staff is clearing away the dishes and the food in the dining room," she said as she placed the tray over my lap and poured my coffee. "Cook wants to know what to do with the dessert dishes in the ice room."

I blinked. *Did we forget to eat dessert?*

"Save it for Francie. I'll probably have the other one." I picked up my orange juice and gulped down the contents of the glass. The cold liquid felt good on my throat, but it made me dizzy all over again.

"I'll relay your instructions." Lillian left the room and I closed my eyes, ever so thankful to be alone.

The strong aroma of the coffee made my head hurt worse, but I drank it anyway, knowing I had to do something to wake up and get moving. I had to go to Mrs. Olson's house this morning and get Julien. Closing my eyes, I sipped the hot liquid and tried to recall what happened last night. Most of the evening escaped my memory, like a fuzzy dream that dissipated the moment I woke up, but I didn't need to remember much to know Will and I had ended up in this bed together. The pillows and blankets bore traces of the unique scent of his cologne.

Suddenly, I realized what a terrible mistake I had made. Will was a man of strong principles and he'd always conducted himself around me with the manners of a perfect gentleman. Inviting him to my home for dinner—and making sure my staff had the night off—probably led him to conclude I was tacitly inviting him to stay the night with me as well.

Wrong...

I cared about his opinion of me and the last thing I wanted to do was degrade myself in his eyes. I never meant to drink so much or act in such a loose manner. There was no way to take back what happened, but could I somehow repair the damage? I drank the entire pot of coffee and ate the Danish roll Cook had warmed for me, racking my addled brain for an idea. One thought kept repeatedly coming back to me; *I must apologize for my behavior.* Excuses would not work with Will. I needed to make him understand that what happened last night was out of character for me.

I eventually talked myself into getting out of bed and spent a half-hour soaking in a nice, hot bath. My condition improved somewhat after that—at least I wasn't shaking anymore—but my head still pounded like the dickens. I dressed and was putting the finishing touches on my makeup when Lillian appeared again.

"You have a phone call, My Lady."

I slowly stood up and pushed back the chair of my dressing table. "Thank you. I'll take it in Gus' study."

I went across the hall and picked up the telephone, hoping to hear Will's deep voice, but to my disappointment, he wasn't on the other end of the line. It was Harv, calling to tell me that he and I were driving up north this afternoon to visit my properties and to let my staff know I'd be gone for several days. He planned to pick me up in an hour. I told him I had to retrieve my son and my sister and got him to push it back to two hours instead. After I hung up, I collapsed in a wingback chair and wondered how I would manage to make it through this trip with a monster hangover.

And without seeing Will for three days…

"My Lady, are you all right?" Gerard stood in the doorway with a concerned look on his face.

I looked up, surprised. I'd been so deep in thought I hadn't heard him come into the room. "Yes, I'm fine. I was just thinking…"

"You have a visitor. I saw the car coming up the drive."

The doorbell rang. I followed Gerard downstairs. It took an effort to talk without wincing.

"Bring them into the library," I said, clutching the banister like a lifeline. I made my way into the library and collapsed into a wingback chair while Gerard answered the door. Covering my face with my hands, I tried to ignore the pulsating pain in my head corresponding with the grandfather clock in the hall chiming twelve times.

"Mister Van Elsberg is here to see you," Gerard said from the library doorway. He moved out of the way for my visitor to come into the room. The familiar cadence of the man's footsteps alerted me to his presence before I saw him. I gasped and looked up.

Will stood in front of my chair holding fresh flowers wrapped in a paper cone, studying me closely. "How are you feeling today?"

"Like I drank too much last night," I said and struggled to my feet, relieved to see him, but at the same time, light-headed from my hangover. I studied him warily, wondering why he looked so chipper when I was dying inside. "I didn't expect to see you today."

He offered me the flowers—a bouquet of large white daisies. "Why not?" He moved close to me, his gaze intensifying. "Is something wrong?"

I laid the flowers on a small drum table next to my chair and looked up at him, mustering the courage to bare my soul. Drawing in a deep breath, I said, "Will, about last night. I need to set the record straight. I should have never consumed so much wine because I did things I never would have done if I'd been sober—"

"Char—wait." He held up his hand, interrupting me. "Look, it's not your fault. I'm the one who needs to apologize," he said gravely. "You're right. We both drank too much, but the blame is all mine because I knew what I was doing was wrong and yet I went ahead with it anyway." He paused, as though collecting his thoughts. "I shouldn't have taken advantage of a woman in your condition."

I should have been relieved that he beat me to the punch with an apology, but deep down it hurt to think I'd simply been no more to him than a drunken mistake. I merely nodded, wondering if this was his way of politely saying "so long and good luck."

"I want you to know, though, I meant what I said last night," he said in a steel-soft tone as his gaze held mine.

My heart began to slam in my chest. "What—what did you say?"

He looked disappointed. "You don't remember?"

I swallowed hard. "No…"

His eyes searched mine. "I've never met anyone who has affected me the way you have. I can't explain it, but ever since that day you stood on my front porch, looking for a job, you've held my heart in the palm of your hand." He pulled me close and spanned his hands around my waist. "I want you to know that no matter what happened last night, I don't think less of you. If anything, you mean more to me than ever now."

My jaw dropped. My eyes filled with tears. I fell against him, burying my face in his chest as snippets of last night began to flit through my mind. "Oh, Will. You don't know how much it means to me to hear you say that. I've been so worried that my actions made you lose all respect for me." I looked up, smiling. "I guess this means we're still friends…"

"Are you kidding me?" He slid his arms around me. "Knowing what I know now, there's no way I could ever go back to the way we were, even if I wanted to. Yeah, we're more than friends, lady. You're stuck with me for good." He began to tickle me and when I struggled to pull away, he dipped his head and kissed me with the same deep passion he'd shown last night. Rising on my tiptoes, I gave myself completely to him, ignoring the fact that the inside of my head felt like a miniature troll was banging on a gong.

"Have dinner with me again tonight," he murmured in my ear. "Only this time I'm taking you out on the town. Showing you off good and proper."

I pulled back. "Oh, I can't," I replied in dismay. "Harv called just before you got here and said he's picking me up in a couple of hours to take me up north. He wants me to visit all of the properties I own. That's the last phase of my training."

He frowned with disappointment and kissed me again. "How long are you going to be gone?"

"At least three days. I'll call you as soon as I get back."

"Three days?" He groaned. "If I don't hear from you by Monday morning, I'll probably be camped on your doorstep when you return."

"Good," I said in a droll voice. "You can keep an eye on Francie for me."

"Ah…" He cleared his throat as he raised his palms. "Sorry, but I don't have any idea how to handle a fifteen-year-old girl."

I snorted in frustration. "Neither do I."

Chapter Nine

I managed to pick up Francie and Julien, get back home, and get packed by the time the Rolls Royce pulled into the driveway. My staff clustered at the front door, bidding me goodbye. Gretchen held Julien and helped him wave bye-bye to me with his chubby little hand. He laughed and tried to grab my hair when I leaned toward him with a farewell kiss.

Francie was conspicuously absent and I assumed she was somewhere in the house, talking on the phone to Elliott. I'd informed her earlier that Gerard was in charge in my absence and she was to obey him or else she would answer tome. As soon as I returned, I vowed to have a talk with Leon Goldman and settle this thing with his nephew.

The drive lasted several hours, giving Harv and me plenty of time to talk on the way. We were staying in a hotel in St. Cloud for the night, then driving on to the towns of Avon and Holdingford on Sunday. On Monday, we would visit my properties in Morrison County before heading home.

As usual, Harv's team of bodyguards followed closely behind us like a permanent shadow.

"There's something you need to know about the tenants of all your properties," Harv said as he poured a refill of Bordeaux into my glass.

"They're poor farmers."

At first, I'd refused to have any wine, but he insisted it would help my headache so I agreed to have one small glass. He was right. The first glass completely took away the pain. The second one settled me down and put me in a mellow mood. "I thought they were moonshine cookers."

"They started out as farmers, but market prices have fallen so much they can't make a living at it. When their farms went into bankruptcy, Gus bought up the properties for pennies on the dollar and allowed the people to stay on as tenants. He got them started in the moonshine business so they could pay their rent and to this day, they remain extremely loyal to him."

I absorbed this information. "Do they know he's dead..."

"Of course," Harv said, "and they've continued to do business with me and Marv as Gus' successors."

"And that's an issue because..."

"Other bootleggers are trying to muscle in on our territory. I want you to assure Gus' people that Marv and I are as trustworthy as he was."

I fidgeted with discomfort. If the brothers were able to keep Gus' territory intact, good for them, but I *did not* want to get dragged into their illegal affairs. I had worked hard to extricate myself from that life and resented being used to promote goodwill to my tenants on their behalf.

My obstinance must have shown on my face because Harv leaned toward me and said, "These are good people just trying to feed their families. Unfortunately, they're getting pressured by someone from St. Paul who merely considers them a stepping stone to making money."

That didn't surprise me. St. Paul was a haven for criminals. As long as they paid their bribe money to local law enforcement and kept their noses clean within the city, whatever crimes they committed elsewhere were their business. Bootlegging was a lucrative industry in Minnesota, particularly in Stearns County. The residents there produced a high-quality, aged product called "Minnesota 13" that had gained national prominence as the best whiskey in the country. Avon and Holdingford were the centers of this high-demand activity—and where most of my properties were located.

Harv adjusted the round, rimless glasses perched on the bridge of his nose. Whenever he did that, I knew he had something important to say. "I would hate to see Leonard Murtagh gain control over your tenants. That would put you in a difficult position," he said gravely. "A difficult position indeed."

I mulled over that information all the way to St. Cloud and the more I thought about it, the angrier it made me. What right did Leonard Murtagh have to hassle my tenants? Who did this bum think he was? Perhaps it wasn't who he thought he *was*, but who he thought he *wanted to be*—the new Gus LeDoux.

I mentally shook my head. Leonard had served as Gus' driver and bodyguard the last year before his death. A mere water boy in the grand scheme of Gus' operation as far as I was concerned. Association with Gus didn't qualify him to become a successful bootlegger! He had to possess a range of the right qualities, many of which he was lacking, in my highly skeptical opinion. Whichever road to hell Leonard Murtagh wanted to take was his business, but he'd better leave me alone—and that included the people who rented from me.

I didn't stress over it again until the next day as we drove to our first farm in Avon Township. As soon as we crossed the county line, the odor of fermenting moonshine filled the air. Wisps of smoke from hidden stills rose above the treetops in the wooded areas we passed.

The private road to the farmhouse, located on a hill, was at least a quarter of a mile long, so the family had plenty of notice we were coming up the driveway. A small pack of dogs chased the Rolls Royce into the yard, barking up a frenzy to announce our arrival. By the time we reached the house, surrounded by tall, shady trees, the Bergmann family stood on the front steps, curiously watching as they waited to receive us.

Marga Bergmann was short and squat in a flowered dress and a beige full-length apron that touched her shoe tops. Her graying brown hair had been twisted into a tight knot at the nape of her neck. Her two sons, in their middle teens, were tall and lanky. Both wore denim overalls. I wondered where Mr. Bergmann was, or if he was still alive.

I liked Marga the moment we were introduced. Though she spoke with a German accent, I understood her perfectly. Gus' right-hand man, Albert Schultz, had spoken with an accent. Over time, my ear had become trained to it and I ceased to notice it.

Marga's home was clean but plainly furnished. It had the aroma of freshly baked bread. "I'm so happy to meet you, Mrs. LeDoux," she said as we sat at the large, square table in her spacious kitchen. Harv drank a stein of homemade beer while Marga and I enjoyed cups of strong, freshly-brewed coffee. "I heard so much about you from Gus when he was alive."

That surprised me, but I could see Gus sitting at this table, drinking beer with this warm, hearty woman.

"I'm sorry about his passing," she continued with a note of sympathy in her voice. "He was a goot man. He helped us when we lost the farm. We owe him so much. I'm sure you miss him as much as I miss my Otto."

I was wondering what had happened to Otto when one of the boys said—

"Papa got three years in Leavenworth for cookin'. He's got a year left."

I gazed at Marga with curiosity. "So, you're in charge of cooking the brew now?"

"Yah," Marga said seriously. "I got to feed these boys."

I was drawn to her courage. "So, you don't farm at all?"

"Farming does not pay what it did during the war. We grow what we need and put the rest of our time into our other business." She set down her coffee cup. "When you only get five dollars for a hundred-pound calf or the same amount for a gallon of moonshine, you know which business you should grow."

"Aren't you worried about Federal agents raiding your operation and going to prison—like your husband?"

Marga shook her head, her expression unapologetic. "Axel and Linus need to be fed and the rent must be paid. I do what I must to care for my family until my Otto comes home."

The strength and resolve of this woman fascinated me. I had no doubt she had faced a bleak and uncertain future when she lost her husband. Her determination to carry on in his absence, despite the obstacles she faced, gave me a deep respect for her.

She gave us a tour of the barn and the rest of the buildings. When she showed us the manmade cave where she kept the still—made from a large copper washtub—she spoke about a man who had visited her and offered her a better deal to sell her whiskey to him. In return, he expected higher production. A man named Leonard Murtagh. It was clear she found the offer tempting, but I could tell she was uncomfortable about dealing with this man.

I couldn't imagine how she'd hang onto her independence if she got mixed up with Leonard. By pressuring her to step up her production, he was already trying to exercise control over her.

As we walked to the car, I told her of my association with the Katzenbaum brothers and attested to their honesty. I also let her know in my sincerest manner how much I enjoyed meeting her and that if she ever needed anything, I'd be glad to help. She indicated that one day she hoped to buy back her farm and I told her I'd hold it until she was able to do so.

"You come to visit me again, Mrs. LeDoux." Then she gestured toward Harv. "I will do business with this man. I trust your word."

She thanked me and then stood in the driveway, along with the boys and the dogs, waving goodbye.

As we drove down the driveway, I realized I'd done just what Harv wanted me to do, but I had no regrets. I didn't condone bootlegging in any way, but at the same time, I didn't blame Marga for doing what she had to do to support her family in tough times. As her landlord and new friend, I felt compelled to do whatever I could to help her.

For the next two days, we visited every one of my properties and the result was the same. As Gus' widow, I gave the brothers a good recommendation and convinced each tenant to continue to supply them with liquor rather than switching their business over to Leonard Murtagh. That said, I had no plans to repeat this process. In the future, my focus was on my own businesses and my family.

I arrived home late on Monday evening and was disappointed when Will wasn't waiting for me as he'd promised. Everything else had gone smoothly, though. According to Gerard, Francie had behaved herself and had been very quiet the entire time. I went to bed tired, but content. Things seemed to be going smoothly—for now, at least. I thought about the last time I saw Will and what he said to me...

I want you to know that no matter what happened last night, I don't think less of you. If anything, you mean more to me than ever now."

I fell asleep with his words locked away in my heart.

*   *   *

The next day, I wandered aimlessly around the house, waiting for Will to call or stop by. The library on the first floor had a small den connected to it and I had chosen to make that room my home office. Both rooms had windows facing the front so I could see when people arrived at the house. I sat at my desk and tried to work, but I couldn't concentrate.

I missed Will so much and wanted to share every last detail with him about my trip up north.

He finally showed up that afternoon. I saw his car rolling up the circular driveway and went out to meet him. I smiled and waved, but as his car came to a stop inside the carriage porch, my breath caught in my throat. I knew instinctively something was wrong—very wrong—because he wasn't smiling back.

Has he changed his mind about me?

Slowly, deliberately, he slid out of the car and shut the door. He walked around the vehicle but didn't advance up the steps to meet me. Instead, he leaned against the car, his hands at his sides, gripping the rear fender.

I held out my arms even as my heart began to thud in my chest. "Will, aren't you going to properly greet me?"

From beneath the black fedora angled on his head, his narrowed gaze surveyed me with barely-suppressed anger. "You lied to me."

I couldn't believe my ears. "What?" I flew down the steps and stood in front of him. "What are you talking about?"

His smoldering eyes penetrated mine. "You've been claiming for months that you wanted nothing to do with bootlegging. And I believed you. So, you can imagine my surprise when I find out that you went up north with Harv Katzenbaum for the sole purpose of promoting his operation to your tenants."

Where did he hear this? I found it hard to believe that Harv would brag to him in that way. It had to have originated from the bodyguards who accompanied us. The men usually sat in their car whenever we visited with a tenant, but if we were outdoors, they'd most likely heard everything we said.

"I—I did talk to my tenants about them," I sputtered, "but it wasn't to promote their business. You've got this all wrong. You don't understand—"

"Yes, unfortunately, I do understand. I should have known all along you wouldn't keep your word. You'll do anything for Harv because he'll do anything for you. You're the daughter he never had. They both adore you. The brothers are probably going to leave all of their money to you and you know that, so naturally, you'll go along with whatever is in their best interests." He paused for a heartbeat. "Even if it means deceiving me."

His words shocked me. I had no idea he felt that way about my relationship with the brothers. It was true, they did treat me like a daughter, but it wasn't true that if I had to choose between them and Will I'd turn my back on him. "Will," I said aghast, "I'd never do anything to deliberately put a wedge between you and me. I convinced my tenants to keep their business with the brothers because I didn't want Leonard Murtagh to take over my properties. It would be like making a deal with the devil himself."

He uttered a mirthless laugh. "You think I don't know everything there is to know about that guy? What do you think I've been investigating since the night he accosted you at the Tansy Club? I've been working exclusively for Harv, digging up everything I could find on what Murtagh has been up to since Gus died. He's gaining more ground every day and he's not going to stop until he's richer and more powerful than Gus."

"What does that have to do with me?"

He tipped his hat back in frustration. "What do you think? You're Gus' widow. The ultimate prize."

Now it was my turn to laugh. "Don't be ridiculous. I'd sooner shoot that crook with his own gun than get tangled up with him."

"You know," he said quietly, "when you invited me here for dinner, I wondered what you saw in me. I'm not rich or connected like the men you're used to dealing with. I'm just an average Joe who helps people solve their problems. I had nothing to offer you that could compare with the level of luxury and privilege you take for granted. But now I know—I was just a toy. An amusing diversion in your busy life."

I clutched my hands over my heart, horrified. "Will, that's not true! You mean everything to me!"

His eyes hardened. "You claimed you didn't want anything to do with bootlegging because it had cost you so much grief, yet the first chance you got, you jumped right back into it with both feet."

"I convinced my tenants not to deal with Murtagh because I had to protect my business interests, not because I wanted to do it." By this time, I was screaming my answers.

"In other words, you care more about the bottom line than anything else." He pinned me with a piercing look. "If you really don't want any more trouble from Murtagh then prove it. Sell those properties. Sell everything you own so you can live your life without always looking over your shoulder."

I thought about Marga and the other good people I'd met last weekend. I couldn't do that to them. Every one of them held the expectation of one day buying back their properties, and in the meantime, supporting themselves the best they knew how until they had the money. I'd made promises to them and if I sold the properties from underneath them, I'd be going back on my word.

"On the surface, it sounds reasonable, but I can't do that, Will. I have obligations to my tenants and my employees. They're people, not numbers on a ledger. Even if I did agree to get rid of everything, life is neither that easy nor that *simple* and you know it."

I tried to place my hands on his chest but he gently pushed me away and tightly folded his arms to keep me at bay. "Then that's *that*," he replied in a stony voice, even though his eyes reflected disappointment and hurt. "You've made your choice."

My heart sank as my mind spun with panic. "There is only one choice for me—you!"

"How convenient to have a boyfriend who can double as your personal bodyguard." He pushed himself away from the vehicle. "Nice try, but I'm not going to lay awake every night, worrying about how to keep you safe, Charlotte, or constantly wondering what else you've lied to me about." He pierced me with a fierce look. "I've always done everything I could to protect you from Gus' enemies but if you won't listen to me now it's because you don't take our relationship seriously. Or care what I think." He turned away. "I'm nobody's fool."

"But…Will! Come back, please! Let's talk this out—" I followed him around to the driver's side, but he ignored me and got into his car. Since the vehicle was still warm, the car performed a hot start without Will cranking it first. He drove away, never looking back.

With tears blurring my eyes, I stood watching as he turned onto Summit Avenue and disappeared. Without meaning to, I had wounded him deeply, but at the same time, I'd hurt myself, too.

I sat down on the steps and leaned my elbows on my knees, covering my face with my hands as I sobbed loudly, upset that life had to be so complicated. It wasn't my fault my late husband had saddled me with his tangled business empire. I didn't choose to inherit his enemies, either, but there I was, forced to deal with both.

My mind drifted back to the day after our dinner date and what Will had said to me in the library.

Knowing what I know now, there's no way I could ever go back to the way we were, even if I wanted to…

His words were still true, but their meaning had changed. They pierced my heart like a shard of glass from a broken bottle of Minnesota 13.

Chapter Ten

I spent the rest of the afternoon in my bedroom, nursing my broken heart. I filled the tub with hot water and soaked for a while, then crawled into bed and buried my head under the covers so no one could see me cry. My staff kept fussing over me, worrying aloud that I might be coming down with something, but deep down, I knew they understood what had made me so glum. I figured somebody probably watched through the window at Will and me interacting inside the carriage porch and *he* told the rest of the staff what happened.

I dressed and went down to the dining room by seven for dinner. Francie seemed to be in an unusually joyful mood, talking nonstop about school and her friends. I sat quietly and listened, preferring instead to concentrate on my food, even though I had very little appetite. I didn't even get upset that she was wearing several shades of my newest palette of eye makeup and had taken one of my favorite hair combs without asking first. We were having coffee and dessert when she looked at me and said, "Don't worry, Char. He'll come back."

I blinked. My fifteen-year-old sister was giving me advice about men? What was this world coming to?

When I didn't answer, she patted my forearm, as if to let me know she understood my dilemma. "He's absolutely in love with you." She nodded seriously. "At the funeral, he never took his eyes off you."

At the funeral? When did my sister have the time to notice Will's reaction to me? She was too busy flirting with Elliott Cohn.

Even so, I found her attempt to cheer me up deeply touching. Given the difference in our ages, I rarely talked to her about my life, but I realized she was growing up faster than I'd anticipated and understood far more than she let on.

I picked up my water glass. "He's not happy with me right now. He thinks I've made some bad business decisions."

She cut off a piece of warm apple dumpling with her fork and stuffed it in her mouth. "It's your business. You can do what you want."

Yes, but...at what cost?

I was trying to formulate a positive response to her comment when Lillian appeared in the dining room. "You have a guest, My Lady. Hal is escorting the person to the door."

It must have been someone who wasn't listed on my roster of approved guests, but I wondered who Hal, my nighttime security guard, would allow on the grounds without checking with me first. I needed to get to the bottom of this...

The doorbell rang and Francie jumped up. "Maybe it's Elliott!" She raced to the front door to see who it was and ran back to me as I reached the library doorway.

"Who is it?"

Francie shrugged, her mouth drooping with acute disappointment. Obviously, it wasn't Leon Goldman's nephew. "I don't know, but she says she knows you and Gus."

That immediately spiked my curiosity. I hurried to the front door and found Adrienne Devereaux standing inside the carriage porch with Hal. He had a grip on her coat and refused to let go. I stared at her, stunned at her worn, faded clothes and unkempt hair—so astonished I couldn't find the right words to greet her. Once upon a time, the raven-haired beauty had performed at La Coquette every weekend. Though she'd had plenty of suitors who'd adored every note she sang, she'd only had eyes for my husband. I'd learned of their affair and confronted them the night La Coquette was raided. She'd remained Gus' mistress, however, until the day he died.

I should have hated her forever, but at Gus' funeral, I decided to make peace in my heart by reaching out to her and even offering her a place to stay. The brothers thought I was crazy to associate with her, but I knew it was the right thing to do.

It appeared she was taking me up on the suggestion.

"She says she knows you," Hal said to me in a tone that suggested he didn't believe it. "I wasn't going to let her in at all, but she swore you'd vouch for her." He glanced at her shabby claret-colored coat with a derisive look on his face. That coat had once been an expensive garment, but difficult times had turned it into a threadbare rag.

"Yes, I know Adrienne," I replied, unable to keep the surprise out of my voice.

"Gus destroyed my career and then left me with nothing. Since you have inherited *everything*, I'm looking to you to make amends," Adrienne declared with a trace of a French accent in her bitter voice. "You once offered me the use of your guest house. Will you honor your word—or now that time has passed, have you changed your mind?"

"Of course, I will honor my word," I stated, surprised at her defensiveness. I had no idea what had happened to her since Gus' funeral, but it was obvious to me she'd been through a difficult time. "Do come in."

Adrienne pried Hal's hand from her shoulder and stomped into the wide-open hall.

"That will be all, Hal," I said. "I'll take it from here."

"Sure thing, Mrs. LeDoux." Glaring at Adrienne with suspicion, he tipped his Fedora to me and started back toward the guard shack.

Adrienne stepped into the house with her hands clasped tightly. She observed the length of the hall, staring wide-eyed at the cut-glass chandeliers and the grand staircase. "So, this is the palace Gus built for you. It's everything I expected it to be." Her bold tone implied that Gus had catered to my every whim.

"May I take your coat madam," Gerard asked politely in his monotone way. He put his hands on her shoulders to remove her garment but the moment he touched her she clutched at the lapels and jerked from his grasp. He stepped back, stiffening as though she'd committed a huge faux pas in the manners department. The sarcastic look in his eyes conveyed in no uncertain terms he considered her rude conduct *typical* of the French.

Adrienne turned to me. "I'm sure you would prefer not to have me impose upon you, Mrs. LeDoux, but I have nowhere else to go. You're my last resort."

"Adrienne, you're most welcome here," I said, noticing how uncomfortable she was. Not many women would have found the courage to come to the widow of a dead lover and ask for help. She must be truly destitute. "Call me Char, please. I'll have my staff go out to the guest cottage tonight and get the heat going so tomorrow they can turn on the water and set it up for you."

"I don't mind a little dust. Or a cold house." She gave me a pleading look. "I'll stay there tonight *s'il vous plaît*."

I sensed the reason she didn't want to stay in the main house was because of her dirty and disheveled appearance. This was definitely not the Adrienne I once knew—a woman who spent more time and money in one week on the way she looked than most women did in a year. Though she tried to mask it with an air of defiance, her shame and

104

humiliation at having to beg me for a roof over her head was palpable.

"All right," I said, getting down to business. I turned to my staff. "Gerard, you're in charge. Have Errol turn on the heat immediately and the water. Stock the cottage tonight—bedding, towels, food—whatever Adrienne will need."

Gerard began to bark orders as my staff left the hall. Errol, the groundskeeper also served as our maintenance man. He occupied a small cottage behind the house as well.

"I need to read a book for class," Francie announced and went upstairs, leaving me alone with Adrienne.

We stood for a moment in awkward silence. "Come into the library," I said to give us some common ground. "Let's have a glass of wine while we wait."

She followed me into the library carrying a small, square valise. It didn't look large enough to hold garments so I assumed it contained what little possessions she had. I offered her a wingback chair, but she declined to sit and I suddenly realized she might be afraid her coat would soil the gold damask fabric. I pulled up two wooden chairs in front of the gas fireplace. We sat down, warming ourselves with our wine. I lifted the glass to my lips, but as the wine's deep bouquet filled my nostrils it made me sick to my stomach. I set the glass on a small table next to me.

Adrienne stared at the fire. "I appreciate your hospitality."

"You're welcome to stay here in the house with me if you prefer." As lonely as I was, I could use her company, even if she wasn't in the best of moods.

She drained her wine. "I've dreamed of living in that little cottage ever since you invited me. I don't want to put you through any trouble. All I ask for is peace and quiet."

I wanted to ask her where she'd been living until now, but realized it would be prying so instead I simply refilled her glass. "If that's what you want, no one will bother you, except to bring fresh supplies. You have my word on that. However, you're most welcome to join me for dinner any time you'd like."

She nodded without giving me a specific answer. "How is your handsome detective?"

I stared at my untouched wine. Now it was my turn to be uncomfortable. "He's unhappy with me at the moment. He thinks I'm getting too big for my britches."

Adrienne laughed. "So like a man! His masculinity is threatened because the woman he loves has dreams of her own."

What makes her think he loves me? He hates me!

She cast me a sideways glance. "Guard your independence with all your heart, *mon ami*."

I appreciated her honesty because I knew she'd experienced losing her independence firsthand when Gus' jealousy had forced her to end her singing career after La Coquette was closed down. His death had devasted her and left her without support. As the person who'd inherited both his money and his property, I was determined to help her get back on her feet. She could have the guest cottage as long as she needed it.

Adrienne drained her glass again and it occurred to me that she was probably hungry. I made a mental note to make sure my staff filled her small kitchen with plenty of food, but for now, I grabbed a tin of cookies off a parlor table and handed it to her. "Shall we have dessert with our wine?"

An hour later, both the cookie tin and the wine bottle were empty when Gerard appeared in the library. "The cottage is still a bit chilly, but otherwise it's ready, My Lady."

Adrienne jumped off her chair and clutched her bag, anxious to be shown to her quarters. As Gerard led her away, I ran upstairs and filled a small box with creams, shampoo, and other personal items. I went back downstairs and took the door to the terrace at the back of the house. As I made my way across the terrace, I glanced across the driveway to the cottage. All of the lights were on and through the window, I saw Gerard standing in the kitchen. I quickly took the stairs and hurried to the cottage before he left. I wanted her to have these things and worried she might become embarrassed when she saw that some of them were expensive. Having Gerard there would create a diversion so I could simply drop the box and leave.

When I arrived, Gerard was explaining the special switch on the wall that would ring a bell in the kitchen in the house. If she needed anything, she was to ring it and one of the staff would attend to her.

"My staff forgot this," I said breathlessly and placed the box on the table. "It's for the lavatory." Gerard gave me a puzzled look as if to differ with me. He glanced in the box and saw an array of my personal items then stood back with a bland expression on his face. No doubt he'd ask about it on the way back to the house, but he had the grace and tact not to say anything in front of Adrienne.

I glanced around. The kitchen had cheery yellow print curtains and a matching tablecloth on a small round table. "I think you'll like this house. It's small, but very quiet back here."

"It's perfect," Adrienne said, the sparkle in her eyes attesting to her approval.

"Don't be a stranger," I said as I walked to the door. "On the other hand, I might just drop in once in a while to visit you and bring some good wine."

She nodded. "You are always welcome."

Back in the main house, I went upstairs and for some odd reason, had the desire to sit in Gus' study. I often felt close to him in there, but tonight I just wanted to rail at him for ruining Adrienne's career. It was such a waste! That woman possessed a deep, smoky voice like no other. When she sang in front of a crowd, dressed in her signature sequins, diamonds, and silk, her sensuality had been mesmerizing. Suitors fell at her feet.

Now, she's wearing rags and begging for a roof over her head.

I angrily gripped the leather arms of Gus' desk chair. How many other careers of the women Gus had slept with had he thoughtlessly destroyed? My mind drifted back to that tattered young girl I'd encountered in front of the Hamm Building several weeks ago. I hadn't seen her since and wondered what had happened to her. What became of other girls in her situation? I'd been homeless once myself—and pregnant. I thanked God I'd been fortunate enough at the time to get hired as Will's housekeeper. Otherwise, my circumstances might have become as dire as that young girl's had and I probably would have been forced to go back to Gus.

"There should be someplace where women who find themselves in unfortunate situations could go for help," I said aloud. "Where they would get food and shelter. A place to start over…with people who care."

I sighed and sat back, staring up at the ceiling when it hit me. The answer had been there all along. I gasped, almost overwhelmed with astonishment as the idea suddenly took shape in my mind. "Of course! That's it!" The spring in Gus' chair creaked as I sat up straight and dropped my feet on the floor. "Why didn't I think of this before?"

La Coquette was sitting empty except for the raccoons who'd taken up residence. That place was big enough to house a fair number of women and it had everything—a kitchen, lavatories, offices, and meeting rooms to convert to sleeping quarters and a large space on the main floor for training. The basement had even more rooms.

The only problem was that I didn't know the first thing about organizing a home for women. Ah, but I knew someone who did…

I jerked open the desk drawer containing Gus' personal phone book and skimmed the alphabet for a specific name. There it was…Oliver Wentworth. He was now an official in the St. Paul Police

Department. Gus used to pay him a handsome bribe to ensure the continued immunity of La Coquette to city laws concerning prohibition. On the other hand, his wife, Sally had a heart as big as the moon and worked tirelessly for a number of causes. If she didn't want to take on this project, perhaps she knew someone who did.

I called the number and reached her right away. We visited for a little while then I told her what I wanted to do and that I'd fund it completely. She quickly informed me that her women's group at church had been discussing the possibility of such a project for a long time. She sounded excited and promised she'd get back to me as soon as she could. I thanked her and hung up then folded my arms and leaned back in the squeaky chair, smiling to myself.

I wonder what Leonard Murtagh will have to say when he finds out I'm turning my gambling den into a home for disadvantaged women.

The thought made me laugh with triumph. I could care less.

* * *

Late April

Mid-morning on a warm, sunny day, I sat in the sunroom, mindlessly leafing through a Vogue magazine and drinking a glass of orange juice when Gerard came into the room with my mail. He set the envelopes in front of me in a neat stack and retreated. I spent another fifteen minutes listlessly paging through the magazine, gazing at the fashions and cosmetic ads.

Since Will and I had gone our separate ways, I'd lost interest in pretty much everything. I went through the motions every day, performing all my required tasks, but my heart wasn't in it. I kept telling myself I didn't need this man to make me whole, but my soul wasn't buying that excuse and it kept grieving because I'd let him down. I'd betrayed his trust by saying one thing but doing the opposite and with *that* man, a mistake of that magnitude was a difficult—if not impossible—situation from which to recover.

With one hand resting on my chin, I flipped through the mail, tossing the envelopes into a messy pile as I scanned the return addresses. Nothing, in particular, caught my eye and I shoved the pile away, plagued with boredom and restlessness.

"Another envelope for you, My Lady," Gerard's deep booming voice echoed behind me.

Disinterested, I turned around and glanced at the square, cream envelope lying on the silver tray in his hand. "Just throw it on top of the pile and I'll look at it later."

Gerard wouldn't budge. "This was delivered in person to the guard shack by a boy who said he was paid to drop it off. Apparently, the sender wanted to make sure you personally received it."

I perked up. Could it be from Will wanting to make amends? With renewed energy, I snatched the envelope off the tray and ripped it open. Gerard responded with his customary bow and retreated from the room as I pulled out a folded piece of heavy stationery and opened it up. It was a hand-scrawled note containing only one sentence.

Sticking your nose where it don't belong could get you killed.

The words stunned me. Who had sent this? Was it some kind of joke? I grabbed the envelope off the table and scrutinized both sides. They were completely blank. The notepaper fell from my hand as I stared out the window at the guard shack, frozen with fear. Having my life threatened was frightening enough, but not knowing who was behind it terrified me. Was Leonard Murtagh behind this? If not, what did it mean?

Calm down. Talk to Harv. He'll help me make some sense of this.

But first, I wanted to talk to Chet, my daytime security guard. I retrieved the letter off the floor and slipped it back into the envelope as I ran down the steps under the carriage porch. I glanced over my shoulder as I walked out to the guard shack, worried the person who penned this threat might be watching me.

The sunny morning had started out a little chilly, but it was noon now and the air was warming up fast.

Chet stepped out of his small building to meet me, a curious look on his face.

I held up the envelope. "Who delivered this?"

He adjusted his dark bowler hat. "A boy, about twelve years old, walked up the driveway and handed it to me. He said to deliver it to you then he ran away."

"You haven't seen him around before this?"

Chet shook his head. "No, Mrs. LeDoux."

Disappointed, I thanked him then walked back into the house and called Harv. He was livid and wanted to examine the note himself. He told me to stay indoors and keep the doors locked until he arrived.

I went around the house and made sure all of the doors were locked, telling my staff I'd heard a report of a burglar in the neighborhood. There was no sense getting *them* all worked up until I knew for sure what was going on.

I went into the library to wait for Harv, but I couldn't settle down. While I waited, I poured myself a glass of aged whiskey. It was a little early to be hitting the bottle, but I needed something to keep my hands from shaking.

I lifted the glass to my lips and took a tiny sip, but the amber liquid burned like molten fire as it slid down my throat, causing me to erupt into a fit of coughing. I spit the whiskey into a potted plant and set the glass on the table. I'd had enough of that stuff. Forever.

Chapter Eleven

I paced the floor for a half-hour before Harv's Rolls Royce pulled into the driveway, followed by his hired posse. Before they had a chance to ring the bell, I met him at the door and ushered the stern-faced man into the library.

"There's not much to the note," I said, shutting the heavy door behind me. I walked into the small den off the library that I used as my office and pulled open the center drawer of my desk. Handing the envelope to Harv, I waited for his reaction.

He pulled out the paper, adjusted his glasses on the bridge of his nose, and stared at the few words it contained. "Whoever did this was an amateur," he said brusquely. "But that doesn't mean we should take it lightly." He stared at the floor, mulling over the situation.

His silence made my shoulders tense with anxiety. "Are you saying it's a real threat? Do you think Leonard is behind it?"

"I don't know," Harv replied, staring at the note again with narrowed eyes, "but I'm not going to take any chances."

He shoved the note back into the envelope and buried it in the inside pocket of his black suit jacket. "I've hired a couple of bodyguards to protect you until we can get to the bottom of who is responsible for the threat. For now, the guards will add an additional layer of security over your property and they'll escort you everywhere you go." He glanced around and I presumed he was looking for Gus' premium liquor stash. I'd had that cabinet emptied and the contents taken to the wine cellar a long time ago. "I'm talking about you *and* your sister," he added. "Don't worry, honey, we'll protect you."

I leaned against the heavy wooden table in the center of the room, hating the idea of having professional guard dogs breathing down my neck once again. I assumed that when I moved back into my house that part of my life was permanently in the past. The tall, spear-tipped wrought iron fence around my property was impossible to scale and I had a guard on duty at the entrance twenty-four hours a day. "Is that really necessary?"

"This is for Francie's well-being, too," Harv said. "You'd better get a couple of beds ready because the men are moving in today."

"Here?" I pushed myself away from the desk. "You expect them to live with us in the house?" I had assumed they'd sleep in the gardener's cottage, eat in the kitchen with the staff, and patrol the grounds when we were home. I wanted to interact with them as little as possible. "I'm not comfortable with having a couple of strange men wandering the hallway outside my bedroom door—or Francie's."

Harv squeezed my shoulder. "They're trustworthy—the best men in the business. I need to have a final word with them, but I'll send them in to get settled before I leave." He gestured toward a thick, ornate door next to the floor-to-ceiling bookcase, obviously to change the subject. "Have you had a chance to go through Gus' things in there?"

"No," I said curiously. "It has two locks and I don't have the keys. I don't know where Gus kept them." I shrugged. "I've looked everywhere and they're nowhere to be found."

To my utter surprise, Harv pulled a heavy, key-laden ring from his pocket and began to open the locks on the door. "I'll get you a new set." He swung the door open to expose a closet-sized bank vault.

I gasped in shock. "I had no idea... I thought this was a liquor closet where Gus kept his collection of imported spirits."

Harv stepped toward the bookcase, climbed up the sliding ladder, and pulled down an old, clothbound book in faded blue from the top shelf. Inside the front flap, he found the combination handwritten in pencil. He worked the dial then pulled the lever and swung open the heavy metal door. Inside were guns, ammunition, and a stack of wooden boxes filled with expensive imported scotch.

Harv pulled out one of the boxes. "I procured these cases for Gus through a friend. May I have one back?"

"Take as many as you'd like," I said. "I have no interest in them."

He took a box and said he'd get more later. Then he bid me farewell and kissed my cheek, but indicated he'd stay in close contact with me to monitor my situation.

After Harv left, I pulled out more crates to see what each one contained. They were mostly sealed cases of liquor—except for one. That one contained several thick bundles of cash and a single bottle of wine with a tag. Curious, I picked up the bottle and read the heavy tag, fastened with a narrow red ribbon. It was actually a small card with a personal note scrawled on it. The note read, "To Adrienne. All My Love, Gus."

Stunned, I stared at the bottle of expensive French wine as the pain of Gus' betrayal washed over me like a flood. My late husband had slept with the woman currently living in the cottage out back as *my guest*. For a fleeting moment, I regretted my generosity, but then I pulled myself together and remembered that Gus had been the villain in this situation, not Adrienne. Even though she'd had an affair with him, she'd been used by him, not the other way around.

The doorbell rang again. I didn't want anyone to see the bottle so I stashed it in my bottom desk drawer along with the cash and went back to restacking the cases. As for the guns, I left them where they were, preferring not to have anything to do with them. I would decide their fate on another day. For now, I needed to find Gus' set of keys to this monster so I could use it to store valuable things of *my* choice.

I'd just finished restacking the last case and shut both doors when Gerard appeared in the doorway of the den.

"You have more visitors, My Lady."

I turned around. "Are they the men Harv hired for extra security?" At Gerard's nod, I said, "They'll be staying indefinitely so they'll need accommodations."

"Shall I put them up in the gardener's cottage?"

"No," I said as I watched surprise register on his normally stoic face. "They'll be sleeping in the house as an additional measure of security."

"Very good. I'll prepare rooms in the men's sleeping quarters downstairs."

His suggestion gave me a much-needed feeling of relief. Lodging for male employees was located in the basement, as far away from my quarters as they could get. I excused Gerard to show the men to their assigned rooms and proceeded to climb the sliding ladder to return the book containing the safe combination to its rightful place on the top shelf of the bookcase. I didn't feel like dealing with my bodyguards yet. The idea of having them underfoot, intruding on my privacy, grated on my nerves, and made me unhappy.

As I slipped the blue book back into place, someone stepped into the den. Irritated, I turned to instruct the bodyguard who hadn't followed directions and gone with Gerard to do so *now,* but the moment our gazes met, I gripped the ladder to keep my shaking knees from collapsing.

Will Van Elsberg stood in the doorway staring up at me and the solemn expression on the lean planes of his face told me he wasn't any happier about this arrangement than I was.

*   *   *

I held onto the ladder with a death grip as I tried to read Will's face, but he kept his true feelings hidden under a mask of indifference. His refusal to show any warmth toward me forced me to do the same. "What are *you* doing here?"

He stared up at me, his manner cool. "Isn't it obvious? Dan and I have been retained to make sure you don't get yourself into worse trouble than you are now."

I glared at him. "I'm not in any immediate danger. Harv said whoever wrote the note was an amateur."

"That's for me to decide." He approached the ladder and extended his hand. "I'm the one entrusted with keeping you safe so I call the shots from now on."

Oh, so that's the way it's going to be…

Feeling mutinous, I turned away and tried to descend the ladder by myself, but my knees were so wobbly my foot caught on a wrung and I almost stumbled. Suddenly, his large hands were spanning my waist and he slowly lowered me to the floor. The gentleness in his touch triggered flashes of intimate memories, filling my heart with so much pain and anxiety I had to breathe deeply to catch my breath. Gripping the nearest wrung to keep myself upright, I turned and said, "Your job is to guard me, not tell me what to do."

He moved in close and stared down at me, confronting me nose to nose. "Let's get one thing straight right now, Mrs. LeDoux. I'm in charge here and I make the rules—not you."

Mrs. LeDoux? Distancing himself by referring to me as someone else's wife hurt me deeply, but I didn't flinch at the words. I could play the game his way if that's what he wanted. Unwavering, I stared back. "Then you're fired."

"You can't fire me." His gaze intensified. "You didn't hire me."

I placed my free hand on my hip. "All it would take is one phone call to settle this."

"Go ahead." He sounded annoyingly confident. "Care to wager on what Harv's response will be? I guarantee you'll lose."

He was right, exasperatingly so! I clenched my jaw. "You're insufferable."

"You're *spoiled*. You've got that old man wrapped around your little finger like a string, but this is one time he won't budge. Neither will I, so your prima donna demands won't work on me. Get out of line and I just might take you over my knee—"

You wouldn't dare, was poised on the tip of my tongue, but knowing that Will was a man of his word, I backed away instead. I had better sense than to test him. "This conversation isn't over," I snapped.

He gave me a bold, decisive look. "It is for me." He turned away and headed for the door, presumably to catch up with Daniel and Gerard.

I fumed at his arrogance.

Despite my resolve not to let on how much he'd hurt me, I simply couldn't watch him leave without asking him why he'd come back. "The last time we talked, you said we were finished because you weren't going to lay awake nights worrying about how to keep me safe and yet here you are, playing chaperone. Bossing me around like a schoolmaster," I shouted at his back. "I'd like to know what changed your mind."

He stopped and looked back, staring over his shoulder. "Yeah, I tried that for a while. Staying out of it. Thinking I could get you off my mind. It didn't work."

Tears spilled from my eyes as I watched him walk away. *If* he still cared for me, he had a strange way of showing it.

* * *

"Set two extra places for dinner," I told Gerard the next time I encountered him in the hall. "Will and Daniel will be joining us tonight." Gerard's look of horror over inviting the hired help to dine with the family prompted me to quickly add, "They need to keep a close eye on Francie."

It's only a little white lie, I thought, *but not altogether incorrect. Francie is going to go through the roof over being supervised when she goes to the library. From now on, she'll have to behave herself around Elliott Cohn.*

"As you wish," Gerard's deep, melodious voice replied.

"And tell Cook to make something tonight from Minnie's recipe book," I said as he made his way to the stairwell the staff used to go to the lower level. He acknowledged my request with a stoic bow and disappeared.

I headed upstairs to lie down for a few hours. I was exhausted.

Lillian came into my room to select a dress for me to wear to dinner. Upon encountering me, she gasped in surprise. She wasn't used to seeing me napping in the middle of the day. "I'm sorry, My Lady. I didn't mean to disturb you. Are you feeling ill?"

"No," I said with a loud yawn, "just tired. It's been such a taxing day already. I'm worn out."

"Goodness, I can understand why." Lillian opened the door to my walk-in closet. "What with that mysterious note showing up and all. I'm glad we have extra security but it still makes one nervous."

Her reply didn't surprise me. My staff often knew the details of important issues before I did. It made sense, though, as their collective eyes and ears probably witnessed a great deal day in and day out while they were going about their duties. They loved to speculate and gossip among themselves. Gerard wouldn't admit that to me on his death bed, but it was easy to get Lillian to share information.

Lillian disappeared into the closet. When she returned, she held a powder blue dress in her hands to be steam pressed. "Would you like to wear this one for dinner?"

I nodded my approval. I was too sleepy to hold a conversation.

Taking the dress with her, she left the room, shutting the door quietly behind her.

I slept most of the afternoon and woke up in time for my afternoon playtime with Julien. He was nearly six months old now and sitting unaided for short periods, but he still preferred to lie on his back and play with his toys.

"Hi, there, Mamma's boy," I crooned as Gretchen handed him to me. I propped him up on my lap. "You're so happy today!"

His first tooth had finally broken through his lower gum. Julien laughed as he opened his mouth wide and drooled onto his shirt. I marveled at how much he'd begun to look like Gus. His wavy golden hair was getting thicker and his eyes had turned grayish-green, like his father's. He had long legs and strong arms. He loved to grab my hair and pull on it, refusing to let go. I had to distract him by tickling his tummy to get him to release his vise-like grip.

While I held him on my lap, I thought about the note that came today. If I was killed, what would happen to my son?

Something in my heart stirred and it wasn't fear. The thought of anyone jeopardizing my son's life in any way drew a surge of protectiveness from deep inside me. My jaw clenched.

I know who the coward is that's threatening me. One day I'll cross paths with Leonard again and when I do…

Julien suddenly kicked his feet and began to laugh. Tucking that thought away, for now, I turned my concentration to entertaining my son. I spent an hour playing with him then I fed him dinner and gave him his evening bath. At six o'clock, I left the nursery to get dressed for dinner.

At seven, I was on my way to the dining room when Francie joined me at the top of the stairs. She stared at me as though I had two heads. "What's wrong, Char?"

I gave her the same look back. "I don't know what you're talking about."

"I'm talking about those dark circles under your eyes. Your face is as white as a sheet. Are you sick?"

"No," I said, irritated. Why was everyone asking me this? "I've got so many problems to deal with right now I'm stressed out!" I gave her a long look to suggest her antics with Elliott Cohn were part of my problem then continued down the stairs.

I need to go to bed earlier, that's all, I told myself. *Stop obsessing over my problems.*

The trouble was that hitting the sack earlier wasn't going to solve the issues facing me or make them easier to bear.

I needed a miracle.

Chapter Twelve

Early May

"I need to go to the bank," I fired at Will, bracing myself for an argument as we stood facing off in my den. The large oak desk between us served as a buffer zone.

Sweeping back the panels of his dark suit coat, he gripped his hands on his hips and shook his head in refusal. "This isn't a good time, Char. We don't know where Murtagh is holed up or how he's planning to carry out his threat against you. Until our sources on the street get some solid leads, we're operating blind."

I leaned across the desk. It had been a week since I received the note and I was going stir-crazy being cooped up in the house. "I can't wait. I need to draw out money for someone and deliver it to her."

His jaw tightened. "Unless it's a life or death situation, it'll *have* to wait. I'm not compromising your safety just to hand off some dough to one of your friends."

I folded my arms to keep my temper under control. I'd learned the hard way that getting upset with Will wouldn't change his mind. This was our second confrontation. Our second test of wills. I didn't win the last one, but I couldn't afford to lose this battle. "The money is for Sally Wentworth. Her church is taking over La Coquette and turning it into a home for disadvantaged women. Someone broke into the building last

121

night and did some major damage to it. Up to this point, the church has used its funds for the cleanup and remodel, but they're running out of resources. Sally needs cash—immediately—or they won't be able to finish the project on time. The grand opening is set for next week."

"Is that so?" he replied, sounding surprised at the fact that La Coquette was undergoing such a drastic change. "Ask Marv to take care of it when he gets back. He has the authority to move money on your behalf."

I shook my head. "Marv isn't due home from Seattle for a couple of days. I need to do this myself. Besides, Sally's anxious to show me how their progress is coming along and she has some issues she needs to address with me concerning the remodel."

I suspected Murtagh was behind the break-in but I didn't have any proof. In any case, I needed to get the money to Sally to hire full-time security to guard the building until it was occupied.

"I'm not letting you out of my sight until I'm satisfied it's safe for you to drive on your own." He reached for the black candlestick telephone on my desk. "I'll give Harv a ring and ask him to do it."

His answer gave me an idea. "But Will," I said softly as I rounded the desk and stopped in front of him, getting close enough to touch him. He straightened and drew in a deep breath, forgetting about the telephone. "I didn't expect to drive myself." I placed my hands on his upper arms and moved close, staring up at him with the most innocent expression I could muster. "I figured *you* would take me there."

He glanced suspiciously at my hands on his arms then back at me. "My car wouldn't provide much protection if someone decided to take a shot at you."

The thought made me shudder inside, but I didn't let it show. "I could call Harv and ask him to send the Rolls Royce to pick us up. It's bulletproof. I'm sure he wouldn't mind lending us his car and driver for an hour or two."

A spark of longing flickered in his eyes before he blinked it away. He hesitated at first, then gently withdrew from my grip. "I'll think about it," he said gruffly. "If Harv doesn't need it this afternoon…maybe. I need to talk to him first. I'm not promising anything."

I let go of him and happily spun away, heading toward the door. "I'm going upstairs to change!" There was no doubt in my mind Harv would send the car to take me wherever I wanted to go.

I sprinted to my room and rang for Lillian. When she arrived, she selected a dress from my walk-in closet and took it downstairs to steam the ruffles on it. In the meantime, I filled the bathtub and soaked in the hot water for fifteen minutes, relaxing the ache in my back from sitting too long in the swivel chair in my den. Normally, going to the bank didn't warrant such a fuss, but it had been a week since I'd left the house and I was bored out of my mind. Besides, I couldn't wait to meet with Sally and see the progress she was making on "Anna's House." I'd renamed La Coquette in honor of my mother.

Forty-five minutes later I came back downstairs. I had on a peach voile dress with a V-neckline and a low-waisted skirt of tiered ruffles. A double row of ruffles cascaded down the front of the bodice. A string of Venetian beads and matching drop earrings completed my ensemble.

I met Will in the hall. "I'm ready to go," I said cheerily, waving my fringed handbag.

He frowned. "You didn't need to get all dressed up to go to the bank."

"A girl never knows who she's going to run into," I said airily as I sauntered past him and watched his frown turn into a scowl. I grabbed my straw cloche hat off the hall table and stood in front of the mirror to adjust it on my head. A linen peach sash circled the hat, tied into a bow in the back, and fastened where the two-inch brim turned up at the nape. I positioned it on my head, taking care not to disturb my soft, marcel waves and wispy finger curls. I checked my orangish-red lips then headed toward the door where Gerard stood, bidding me goodbye.

I walked out into the warm sunshine and took a deep breath of fresh spring air. A lot had changed in the last week. The trees were budding, lilies were poking through the soil and the daffodils were blooming.

The Rolls Royce was parked inside the carriage porch and the chauffeur stood conversing with Daniel. I bounced down the steps, happy as a lark to get out of the house, and waited for the chauffeur to open the car door for me. Will followed me outdoors and slid in next to me. Daniel slid into the front seat.

On the ride to downtown St. Paul, Daniel and Will kept watching to make sure we weren't being followed. When we arrived at the bank, a long, narrow structure next to the Endicott Building, Will and Daniel both emerged first and swept the area for any signs of trouble. I waited in the car for permission to leave, wondering if all this extra precaution was necessary. If no one had followed us downtown, how would anyone know we were here? I kept my thoughts to myself to avoid an argument and climbed out when Will motioned that the coast was clear and opened the door.

"Go quickly and when you're in the bank, don't talk to anyone," he said in a low voice as he walked me to the entrance. "Take care of business and come back out immediately. Understand?"

"Of course." With a nod, I clutched my purse tightly and proceeded into the bank. Luckily, I found a teller with no customers and got my money quickly. I turned around to head back to the car, anxious to hand the fat envelope of currency over to Sally Wentworth when I stopped short. Elliott Cohn stood at an adjacent teller, scooping up his withdrawal of cash and having a lively conversation with the man. He didn't notice me as I looked their way, observing their joking around. Judging by the happiness in his voice, Elliott was looking forward to a wild weekend.

"Sounds like you're really dizzy over this dame," the teller said.

Elliott grinned as he pulled out his wallet. "My favorite squeeze!"

"Is this the one who calls you all the time?"

"You mean, the blonde?" Elliott shoved the cash into his wallet. "Nah, she's just for laughs."

I knew exactly who he meant by *the blonde*. Incensed, I turned away, wondering if I should wait for him. I wanted to give him a piece of my mind about the way he was casually using my sister.

It probably won't do any good. I doubt this punk would listen to me.

The only person he *might* listen to was his Uncle Leon.

I looked around and saw a side exit that led to an alley between the bank and the Endicott Building. A security guard sat on a stool next to the door, monitoring the customers who came and went through that entrance. I knew Leon had an office somewhere downtown and if it was next door, it made sense that he would do his banking here. And his nephew. If I went out that side door, I could hurry around to the back of the building, run in and check the directory to see if Leon had an office there. If not, I would come right back.

Guilt plagued me as I glanced toward the front door. Did I have enough time to sneak over there and talk to Leon? My business had concluded rather quickly so perhaps…

I opened the side door and peered out to see if anyone— specifically a parked car that could belong to Murtagh—was in the alley.

It was deserted.

I went through the door and scurried down the short alley to the back of the Endicott Building. The back entrance was unlocked so I hurried inside and went into the lobby. Running my finger down the directory, I found what I was looking for; Leon Goldman's office was located on the tenth floor.

The only available elevator stood empty. "Tenth floor please," I said to the elevator operator. The white-haired woman extended her gloved hand, pulling the glass door and metal scissor gate closed then pulled the lever down on the manual control. The elevator slowly glided up to the tenth floor. As soon as she stopped the car and opened the door, I stepped out, looking for Leon's office. To my dismay, I couldn't find it among the offices on that floor. A door at the end of the long hall had no name painted on the yellowish pebble glass.

I hope that one is his. If not, I'm out of options.

I pushed open the door and encountered a woman about my age with short, reddish hair wearing a green print tunic top and a solid pleated skirt. She stood by the window, watering her spider plant. She stopped, holding a small gray watering can with a long spout in midair. "May I help you?"

I shut the door behind me. "Is this Mr. Goldman's office?"

She set down her watering can and glanced toward the noise. "Yes, but he's in a meeting." Her gaze swept over me with a critical eye. "And you are…?"

A round of raucous laughing thundered behind the closed door to Leon's office.

"Charlotte LeDoux," I said. "I must speak to him right away. It's urgent."

Her expression changed the moment she recognized the desperation in my voice. She gave me a derisive look. "That's what they all say." She pointed toward a small notepad on her desk. "Leave your number. If it *is* important, he'll call you back."

Another burst of laughter exploded in Leon's office.

"I haven't got time for that," I said impatiently, discarding my manners as I moved toward his office door. "I need to talk to him *now*."

"Hey," she shrieked as I turned the knob and burst into Leon's office." I said you can't go in there—"

Leon Goldman relaxed behind his desk smoking a smelly cigar and resting his feet on an open drawer. The moment he saw his door open, a feral look crossed his rounded, middle-aged face. His feet slipped off the drawer and hit the floor with a heavy thud. He tossed his cigar into an ashtray and slipped his hand inside his coat.

Within a split second, I heard the scraping of chair legs on the floor as all three men in his company sprang to their feet. I nearly fainted at the hair-raising *clicks* of the hammers being cocked on their revolvers.

"I'm sorry, Mr. Goldman, I couldn't stop her. She just barged right past me—"

Leon motioned with a jerk of his head toward one of the men. The one closest to the door, a short guy dressed in a gray suit, sprang into action. Still holding his gun, he immediately checked the secretary's office and then peered out into the main hallway. "Coast is clear," he said coming back into the room.

Leon removed his hand from inside his coat and relaxed again. "Never mind, Maisie. I'll handle this. Just shut the door behind you."

I didn't like the fact that three weapons were still pointed at me. "I'm not armed so you can put down your guns, gentlemen."

The middle one, a handsome dark-haired guy sporting a day's beard growth gave me an insolent grin. "Which gun?"

The trio busted out laughing at his obvious joke about a certain part of his anatomy. Unimpressed, I turned back to Leon to get this over with, but he didn't seem to be in any hurry. The corners of his mouth edged upward as his coffee-colored eyes quickly assessed every curve on my body—in detail. "Good afternoon. Is this a social call, *Mrs.* LeDoux or are you here on business?"

I didn't know if the way he emphasized the word *Mrs.* was supposed to be a compliment or another joke at my expense. In any case,

I glared at him, hoping my false show of bravado would make him take me seriously. "A social call? Far from it, *Mr.* Goldman," I said crisply. "You and I need to discuss your nephew."

"Why?" Leon's thick dark brows furrowed. He picked up his cigar and a lowball glass filled with amber liquid. Probably some of his best bootlegged whiskey. "What did that little—what did he do now?"

"He's carrying on with my sister behind my back."

Leon's sense of humor returned, regarding me with a chuckle. "And that's what you're in such a tizzy about?"

I gripped my hands on my hips. "You bet it is. I want it to stop. Immediately!"

He shrugged. "I don't know anything about it. I don't pay much attention to the kid. Keeping him in line is my wife's job. I'm just puttin' up with him until my sister gets back from her trip."

"Then I suggest you *start* paying attention to him from now on," I said, poking Leon in the chest with my finger, "because if you don't and I have to step in, he's going to be one sorry young man after I get through with him."

Instead of showing concern—as I'd hoped—Leon's face widened with an incredulous grin. He set down his glass and grabbed my hand, refusing to let go. "You're going to do a number on him, eh? Pretty tough talk for such a little thing." After I jerked my hand away, he straightened in his chair and gave my five-foot-two-inch frame another quick once-over. "You must be all of a hundred pounds soaking wet."

I weighed a hundred and ten pounds, but that was none of *his* business. "Look, my sister is only fifteen. This is her first romantic involvement with a boy and she's absolutely star-struck over your nephew. We both know that's a prescription for disaster."

Leon dismissed my concern with a wave of his hand. "So, a couple of kids are smoochin' in the back seat of a Flivver. So what? It ain't hurting anything."

I stared pointedly into his eyes. "If Elliott's intentions are honest, why is he sneaking around with her behind my back? What's he afraid of? Why doesn't he come to the house to see Francie? And ask my permission to take her out?"

Leon snickered. "Maybe he's afraid of *you*."

That got a round of belly laughs from the Three Musketeers warming the chairs behind me. *And it made me mad.* My sister's reputation was nothing to joke about—or her virtue. I was determined to spare her from the hurt and humiliation of making the same mistake with Elliott that I'd made with Will.

I placed my hands on his desk and leaned forward, meeting him nose-to-nose. "I promised my Mamma I'd watch out for Francie and I'm not going to let Anna down. You tell Elliott for me to get his hands off my little sister and keep 'em off. If he pulls any shenanigans on her or gets her in *any* kind of trouble..." I leaned closer. "...I swear, he'll regret it."

A chorus of oohs and aahs echoed from the peanut gallery.

The corners of Leon's eyes crinkled. "My, but you're quite the spitfire, aren't you? You sure are cute when you're mad. I can see why Gus was so jealous of you."

I didn't know anything about my spunkiness being a source of Gus' jealousy, but I did know I'd had enough of Leon's annoying banter. I perched my hip on the edge of his desk and braced myself with the palm of my hand. "Yes, well, dynamite comes in small packages."

His piercing gaze rose from my cleavage to my eyes. "Baby, I'd love to light *your* fuse."

The room exploded with laughter, but instead of fuming over it, I suddenly realized I could use this moment to my advantage. Leon could have thrown me out for bursting in uninvited. Instead, he'd listened to my problem and although he'd found it profoundly amusing to make me lose my temper, I instinctively knew he would do as I asked. He had a rather irritating way of showing it, but he genuinely liked me.

You just don't know, do you? The effect you have on men…

Will's words echoed in my head, convincing me to play along. "Shame on you," I said, lowering my voice to sound pouty. "You know I'm not that kind of girl…"

The room went silent. Leon's brows shot up, but for once, he didn't know how to respond.

My gaze slid to the three goons staring at me, speechless at my remark. I slid off the desk and sauntered toward the door. Gripping the doorknob, I turned around. "I expect you to do the right thing. Otherwise, *I'll be back.*"

Leon leaned back in his chair and chewed on his cigar. "I'm counting on it, sweetheart. The door's always open for you."

"That's good to know." I pulled open the door and a wave of refreshing air engulfed me. I hadn't realized until now how stuffy it had become in that room. On second thought, it was inevitable with all the hot air blowing around in there.

"Charlotte…"

The grave tone of Leon's voice caught me unaware. Puzzled, I stopped and looked back.

The serious, focused look on his face indicated he wasn't kidding any longer. "You should have bodyguards with you at all times," he said gently. "If you was my wife, I wouldn't let you out of my sight without protection, but you're not so I don't have any say over it. Since Gus isn't around anymore to keep the wolves at bay, let me give you some friendly advice. Get yourself some professional reinforcement."

"Thank you. I appreciate your concern," I said honestly. "I do have bodyguards, but I didn't bring them with me. I didn't think they'd be welcome on your turf. Goodbye."

Maisie stood behind her desk, staring at me as I left the office. No doubt she'd heard every word of the conversation. Once out in the hallway, I quickly shut the door behind me and ran to the elevator bank. Because I was short on time, the elevator seemed to take forever to arrive at the tenth floor. When the door opened, I scurried inside. "Lobby, please," I said to the operator. As luck would have it, the elevator stopped on one floor after another. By the time it reached the lobby, apprehension had caused the back of my neck to sweat. I didn't know how long I'd been gone, but it was probably long enough to arouse Will's suspicion.

Come on, elevator. I'm in a hurry!

The elevator door opened and I followed the crowd out of the car then took off toward the back door. I exited the building and sprinted around the corner. And came to a dead stop.

Will was in the middle of the alley, walking straight toward me. The murderous look on his face made my heart skitter. I'd pushed him too far this time...

*   *   *

Will swiftly approached me and gripped my arm. He hustled me to the car, his jaw clenching, his face turning a deeper shade of crimson with each step.

I should have known it would take too long...

Daniel approached the car. "Oh, you've found her. Was she in the bank all this time?"

Will merely glanced at Daniel as he opened the door for me to get into the back seat, but I hesitated before getting inside. "Look, I can explain—"

"Just get in the car," he said in a low voice and glanced around, scanning the area for signs of trouble.

I slid in and moved as far to the other side of the seat as possible. He slid in after me and didn't seem to notice the chasm between us. He sat rigid, watching everything but me, his lips pursed. It took a lot for Will to get upset, but when he did—look out.

He was cold and distant all the way home. Needless to say, I didn't bring up the subject of stopping off at Anna's House. I'd decided to ask Errol to deliver the envelope for me. I could talk to Sally on the phone about the ongoing progress.

As soon as the Rolls stopped under the carriage porch, Will got out and opened the car door himself instead of waiting for the chauffeur. He assisted me then took me by the hand and led me past Gerard who stood at the front door, welcoming us home.

Inside the house, Will pulled me into the library and shut the door. "I told you to come straight back to the car," he said, his voice smoldering with fury. "Where did you go?"

"I came across Elliott Cohn in the bank and—"

His gaze bored into mine. "I said, *where did you go?*"

"To Leon Goldman's office—"

"Why?" His eyes blazed. "Was this something you'd planned to do all along?'

"No, of course not."

"Then why didn't you listen to me?"

"This was important!" I shot back. "I needed to talk to Leon about his nephew taking advantage of my sister. I told Leon I wanted it stopped."

"What in the world were you thinking?" Will pulled his hat off and tossed it on a chair. "Murtagh and his men could have been waiting in that alley to ambush you! Or kidnap you!" He thrust his hands into the air in frustration. "If Goldman was behind the threat, you'd have never made it out of that building alive!"

"Not Leon." I shook my head, certain of that. "If he had a problem with me, he'd have shown up at the house in person and threatened me to my face, not hidden behind an anonymous note."

Will towered over me. "What you did was reckless and it could have been fatal. When you didn't come out of the bank, I started to get worried. I couldn't find you anywhere. I was afraid someone had abducted you."

He was so close I couldn't breathe. I took a step backward to put some space between us and smacked my back against the door. Instead of backing away, Will braced his hands against the door on both sides of me, pinning me. Dipping his head, his lips brushed my ear. "How can I protect you when you won't cooperate?" The pleading in his voice startled me.

I hadn't set out to make his job difficult, but his question made me realize that's what I was doing. I looked up and as our gazes locked, the despair in his eyes saddened me. He was hurting over our breakup as much as I was but it was my stubborn, independent attitude that was keeping us apart.

I'm too headstrong for my own good—too much of a spitfire.

I placed my hands on his chest, desperate to make amends. My heart ached with longing for us to be close again. "I'm sorry," I whispered. "I was wrong and I won't ever do it again." Raising on my tiptoes, I looked into his eyes, silently imploring him to kiss me and make up.

Instead of taking my cue, he pulled back, his stony face once again masking his true feelings. "Don't ever disobey my orders again, Charlotte. Do you understand? My job is to protect you, not cater to your whims."

Upset by his swift reversal, I wrapped my arms around my midriff and fought back the lump swelling in my throat. "I promise, Will. I mean it. From now on, I'll do this for you."

He glared at me. "Do it for yourself. Someday it just might save your life."

He pushed me aside, jerked open the door, and walked out without looking back.

Chapter Thirteen

Dinner was a tense affair. Will and I sat next to each other, but we barely spoke. He seemed preoccupied so I didn't try to start a conversation with him. After the upsetting exchange we'd had this afternoon, I didn't know what to say. He never came back to retrieve his hat, sending Gerard after it instead.

After dinner, I went into the den to pen a letter to my renter and new friend, Marga Bergmann, to keep in touch with her like I'd promised I would, but I couldn't concentrate. My head pounded and my heart simply wasn't in it. Not tonight, anyway.

I stood up and rubbed my aching back. "I've got to get a better desk chair," I grumbled to myself. "This one is crippling me."

Exhaling a bored sigh, I wandered to the window and gazed out, scanning the front of my property. It was dark out, but the window in the guard shack glowed brightly. I stood gazing at the golden light when I saw a silhouette appear at the door of the shack. After a few moments, it opened and the person went inside.

Curious, I watched for a while, wondering what was going on, but I couldn't see the details from so far away. I went into the library and grabbed a pair of binoculars off a high bookshelf then went over to the window and held them up to get a better look at the activity in the shack.

Through the window, I observed two people drinking coffee and enjoying a lively conversation—Hal and Adrienne. I knew she took daily walks around the grounds to get some fresh air, but this was the first time I'd seen her interact with anyone.

"Well, I'll be darned," I mused. "Those two have become friends."

I remembered how wary and distrustful they'd been of each other the night Hal had escorted her to the house, disbelieving her claim that I would vouch for her. Lonely and destitute, Adrienne needed friends and I was glad to know she and Hal had settled their differences.

I put the binoculars away and went into the sunroom to cuddle under a blanket on the chaise lounge and listen to the radio for a while. I must have fallen asleep for the next thing I knew, Lillian was shaking me awake.

"My Lady," she said frantically, "Hal is on the back terrace, holding an intruder! Will needs you to come right away!"

Will needed me? I scrambled off the chaise lounge but my mind was so disoriented I lost my balance and nearly fell. Lillian screamed, catching me before I took a tumble on the shiny wood floor.

"No need to worry. I'm fine." I felt silly about my lack of coordination. "I shouldn't have tried to get up so fast."

She walked me through the hall to the back entrance. Gerard was standing outside the door and opened it for us. A rush of cool evening air enveloped me as I stepped onto the terrace.

What in the world...

The entire staff had congregated on the terrace to see the intruder. Adrienne was there, too, but she stood off to one side by herself, taking in the scene. I had no idea where Francie was, but I assumed she was either studying or on the telephone; most likely the latter.

Daniel had grasped the man by the scruff of his neck, holding him down as he cursed loudly and fought to get free. The terrace lights shone brightly upon the area and when I saw who had somehow breached my security, I stared in disbelief.

The intruder was none other than my father, Floyd Johnson.

Hal approached me, his expression grave. "I'm sorry, Mrs. LeDoux. When I opened the gate for Errol to drive through, the man ran inside behind the car."

I walked over to my father, scrunching my nose. He looked worse than he did at Mamma's funeral. And smelled just as bad. My staff kept their distance as they watched the scuffle with curiosity. The looks on their faces showed they had no idea who he was, but of course, Will and Daniel knew.

Papa thrashed about, trying to get away. "Charlie, tell yer hired gun to get his hands offa me!"

Will gestured to Daniel to release Papa. The moment Daniel let go of Papa's filthy shirt, Papa tried to take a swing at Daniel but he missed and almost lost his balance. Daniel grabbed him again to keep him from fighting.

"Stop it!" I snapped. Standing at a distance, I couldn't tell if my father was drunk or sober but knowing him, he'd most likely been tipping his share of drinks before he showed up here. "Why did you try to sneak in? What do you want?" The question was a waste of breath because I already knew why he'd risked getting himself shot trying to get past Hal. I asked anyway.

Daniel released his grip. Papa straightened up and stumbled toward me. "I'm hungry but I ain't got no money." Will extended his arm, barring Papa from getting any closer. "I was hopin' you'd spare your old man a coupla fins to tide me over 'til I can find some work."

I sighed. Of course, I'd give him money. I always did even though I knew his first two purchases would be a "deck of Luckies" to smoke and a fruit jar of hooch to drink. I'd give him some cash and he'd disappear again, probably for months. All he cared about were his cronies and his vices.

"All right," I said slowly. "I'll be right back." I sounded tired, but in truth, I was emotionally worn out. I couldn't handle another crisis—at least not today.

Papa strained behind Will's outstretched arm to approach me again. "If ya don't mind, can ya put me up for the night, too? Gimme some supper?"

I started to speak when Will's gaze cut to mine, stopping me mid-sentence. He walked toward me and stood with his back to everyone. Daniel took Will's place next to Papa. "Char, I realize you want to help your father," Will said, "but he can't stay. I'm sorry. We can't trust him. Someone could have paid him to breach security so he could get in and look around—go over the layout of the house."

Will's adamant response surprised me even though I understood his reasoning. Leonard could have paid my father—who was always broke and looking to make an easy buck—to get inside the house and gather information about the staff and security. Nevertheless, the man was my family. "I understand, Will, but you know this puts me in a difficult position," I said quietly, not wanting Papa to hear me. "I feel guilty about turning away my father."

"Given the present situation, it can't be helped." He squeezed my arm. "I'll talk to him."

I went into the house to get some cash for Papa while Will broke the news to him. In the den, I opened the bottom drawer of my desk and pulled a handful of twenties from one of the bundles of money. When I returned to the terrace, my father stood in between Daniel and Will. I handed him the cash, knowing he'd head toward the first speakeasy he could find and commence to squander the entire wad. It made me sad, but I couldn't refuse to help him.

"Is this any way to treat yer own pa?" Papa snatched the money away from me and then spat a glob of chewing tobacco on the flagstone. "I 'spose I ain't good enuf to come inside yer fancy house!"

Bewildered by his sudden outburst, I clasped my hands together. "But, Papa, I've given you enough money to stay in a hotel for a month and buy meals, too. Why are you upset? Isn't that the reason you're here?"

"Maybe I wanted ta see Francie and hold my grandson," he hollered as Daniel grabbed him by the arm and pulled him toward the stairs. "Or are they too good for me, too?"

I turned to Will as the brunt of Papa's words seared my conscience. He'd only seen Julien once since the baby was born and that was for a brief period during the funeral reception. Sadly, it never occurred to me that he'd want to see his only grandchild again.

"Wait!" Adrienne stepped forward holding up her hand. She wore a long red shawl that had been left in the cottage by a previous guest. "I have a suggestion. If you approve, I'll put him up in my quarters for the night. The cottage is small, but tomorrow, he can have the use of my living room to spend some time with Francie and the baby before he takes his leave."

Stunned by her offer, I stared at Will to gauge his reaction. He didn't answer at first, giving me hope that he was weighing the possibility. I followed him as he walked toward Adrienne, keeping his back to the group. "Are you sure you want to do this?" he whispered to her. "He reeks worse than a dead skunk."

"I can handle him. I'll clean him up and cook a meal for him." Adrienne shrugged. "It's the least I can do to repay Char for what she's done for me."

Will looked her straight in the eye. "I'll approve this on one condition. He does *not* leave that cottage all night. I don't want to see him wandering around the grounds. He stays in your care until he's ready to leave. Understand?"

"Yes," Adrienne replied with a nod. "I understand."

"Fine." Will gave his consent with a wave of his hand. "Escort him to her place, Dan."

"Thank you," I called to Adrienne as she and Daniel disappeared down the terrace steps with my father. "I'll be over with Francie and the baby in the morning."

The rest of us made our way back into the house. Will walked beside me. "Dan and I'll take shifts tonight, patrolling the grounds to make sure we don't get any more unwanted visitors."

My heart sunk to my toes. My life had become so unsafe that even my own father wasn't trusted to visit me. Could things get any worse?

"Thank you for letting Papa stay," I said to Will as he opened the door for me. Instead of walking inside, I moved close and placed my hands on his chest. "And thank you for all you do to keep my family safe. I don't know what I would do without you."

"We need to talk," he said as we entered the hall. "Let's go into the library."

*   *   *

I dutifully followed Will across the hall and into the library. My breath caught in my throat when he shut the door. I sensed he had something important to say, but I didn't dare guess as to what was on his mind. The last time we met to talk in here, it had ended badly. This time I hoped we could put our differences aside and become close again.

Gerard lit the fireplace in the library every evening at dusk when the nights were cool. I stood staring at the soft orange and gold flames as I waited.

"I don't know how to tell you this without upsetting you," Will said solemnly as he stood facing me, "so I'm just going to speak my mind. It's obvious you haven't given up on us, but it's time you acknowledged the truth, Char. The issues that separate us are greater than what binds us together. You need to accept that it's never going to work out between us. When this job is done, we're going our separate ways."

What?

As he correctly predicted, my heart began to break. I had sensed a change was coming, but I'd never expected this…

"Will…" I found it difficult to speak as I blinked furiously to keep tears from flooding my eyes. "No relationship is perfect. We can make it work if we try. We're meant for each other."

He let out an exasperated sigh. "Charlotte, don't make this any harder than it is—"

"I know you care for me," I cried. "That's why you came back and why you admitted you were worried about me. I wish you would listen to reason."

Light from the fire illuminated his troubled expression. "Face the facts, Char. Wishing isn't going to change who we are. We come from completely different worlds. I'll never fit into yours and I have no right to ask you to give up all of this for me." He held up his hands and gestured toward the crystal chandelier suspended from the ceiling to point out that we were surrounded by the opulence of *my* Summit Avenue mansion. "Gus set a course for your life that's impossible to escape and your present troubles are solid, indisputable proof of that."

"I'm a bootlegger's *widow*, Will," I argued. "That way of life died with Gus. It has nothing to do with me anymore. You know how much I detest that business."

"So you say, but it's still very much alive with Harv Katzenbaum and as long as he's a central part of your life, you'll be pulled back into it deeper and deeper until something disastrous happens."

"That's not true! I'll talk to Harv and—"

He closed his eyes for a moment as if steeling himself against giving in to his true feelings. "When I found out you'd gotten involved with the Katzenbaum brothers' bootlegging operation, I knew our relationship didn't stand a chance. As long as you had one foot in their camp and one in mine, you'd always be caught in the middle."

My heart sank. "Will, you're wrong. I've never compromised my values. I'm not involved in any of Harv's illegal activities and I know he'd never ask me to do anything that would endanger me. I simply told my tenants he and Marv were men they could trust."

"I believe you, but the trained investigator in me recognizes you're too close to him to know when to draw the line." He took my hand. "Look, we're like night and day, Charlotte. You're headstrong and fearless—sometimes to the point of recklessness. In my line of work, I've learned to be cautious and thorough because my life depends on it. If we were together, I'd be so anxious all the time about keeping you safe that it would drive me out of my mind. I couldn't live like that. Neither could you. It's best to leave things as they are."

Then he was gone.

I stared at the closed door, numb with shock. In a fleeting moment, the course of my life changed forever. When Mamma died, I'd experienced the most profound sense of loneliness I'd ever known, but that had been a mere scratch compared to this.

I needed to get out of this room—away from the lingering scent of Will's cologne and the memory of his last words. I needed fresh air and a change of scenery. Swinging the door wide open, I drew in a deep breath as I walked into the hall and went up the split staircase to my bedroom. Lillian was leaving my room as I arrived.

She smiled. "I've lit the fireplace and turned down your bed. Would you like some tea before you retire, My Lady?"

I nodded numbly and went into my bedroom. I kicked off my shoes and plumped the pillows then lay on the bed, reclining against them.

Guarding the Bootlegger's Widow

My life is in such a dismal state. What am I going to do now?

Wiping tears from my eyes, I thought about that for a few moments. Then I realized something—a sobering pattern in my life. When Mamma was alive, her unconditional love had given me the strength to keep going. When she died, I'd turned to Harv and Marv—until Will came along. All I had ever wanted was independence. So why did I keep depending on other people to fortify me?

Because I want to love and be loved. I don't want to be alone...

Independence, however, had nothing to do with love and had always been mine for the taking. I'd simply never realized how much control I'd always had over my own destiny.

I let out a deep sigh and stared at the ceiling. How did a woman who only stood five feet and two inches tall successfully make her way in a man's world? The answer seemed obvious. Beat the men at their own game by outsmarting them.

But, how?

I pondered that question—which led me to another one. *What would Gus do?*

My late husband had exhibited the sexual morals of an alley cat during the latter part of our nine-year marriage and had taken many secrets to the grave, but his exceptional skills as a businessman and a leader had made him one of the most powerful men in St. Paul. If Gus was still alive, what advice would he give me? In my mind's eye, I envisioned the rugged lines of his face, his sandy-colored hair, and his penetrating green eyes. The answer came to me almost immediately.

Always be one step ahead of your enemies...

Lillian arrived with my tea. She set the tray on my nightstand and poured a cup for me before bidding me goodnight. I sat up, gazing at the calming fire, and sipped the hot, fragrant liquid. Dynamite really did come in a small package and I was determined to prove it.

"Look out world," I said, quoting Will. "Here comes Charlotte LeDoux."

*   *   *

The next morning after breakfast, Francie and I descended the terrace steps to visit our father at Adrienne's cottage.

"I don't know why we're bothering," Francie grumbled. "He's never gone out of his way to see us. He never even came to the house to see the baby when Julian was born. His only grandchild!"

Nevertheless, she'd put on a low-waisted teal dress and fixed her hair. My pearl and rhinestone barrette looked good fastened behind her ear and I told her so, even though she hadn't asked my permission to use it.

I gripped the handrail, careful to take each step slowly. Julien was growing by leaps and bounds and becoming so heavy I could hardly carry him. My arm ached by the time we reached the cottage.

Adrienne opened the door and came out to greet us. She still wore the dress she had on the night she arrived, but my staff laundered and pressed it for her every morning. Her short, raven hair gleamed like obsidian in the morning light. "Please, sit down." She motioned toward the outdoor furniture. "I'll be back in a minute." Her cottage was too small to entertain so many people and she'd had the staff bring the heavy outdoor furniture down from the terrace. She disappeared into the cottage and reappeared a few minutes later with coffee service on a tray. Papa followed her holding a plate of freshly baked cookies.

I don't know whose mouth gaped open wider—mine or Francie's, but we both stared at the amazing new version of our father. True to her word, Adrienne had forced Papa to bathe and shave. She'd even trimmed his hair. I didn't know what she'd done with his filthy clothes, but he now wore a green striped shirt and a pair of dark trousers with suspenders. On second thought, it looked like clothing I'd seen Errol wearing before, but I didn't say a word about it. Neither did Francie.

"There's my boy," Papa said with a twinkle in his eyes and a grin as his gaze fell on Julien. He set down the plate and held out his arms. "Come to your Grandpa."

I fully expected Julien to burst into tears, but instead, he sat on Papa's lap and became engrossed in his treat when my father fed him small, soft pieces of a cookie. Julien's first teeth had recently come through—the two bottom ones in the front, but we kept an eye on him to make sure he didn't choke on his food.

I glanced at Adrienne, wanting to know how she'd accomplished overnight what our family couldn't do in twenty-five years, but she only smiled back.

We drank our coffee and nibbled on cookies as we watched Papa play with Julien. Francie and I were too astonished to speak. Adrienne kept checking her wristwatch. She seemed to be waiting for something.

Julien began to yawn, a sure sign it was time for his morning nap. Before I could take him, he fell asleep on Papa's lap.

"Floyd," Adrienne said boldly, "it's time." She turned to Francie and me. "Ladies, your father has something to say to you."

Francie and I stared at each other and froze, waiting for a bombshell to drop.

Papa stared at the scuffed toes of his worn shoes. It took him a full minute before he finally spoke. "I'm sorry for what I've put you girls through. All my years of boozin' and..." His voice wavered. "...fer abandonin' yer ma." He swallowed a sob. "My sweet Anna. I miss her..."

I turned my head and stared at Francie again to gauge her reaction. The stunned look in her eyes described exactly what I was thinking: *Where did this come from? Was it even real? Why now?*

Francie's stone-faced expression and pursed lips projected her disbelief in Papa's sudden and unexplainable change of heart. "Does this mean you're going to quit drinking?"

Papa looked at us. "I'm goin' to try. You girls are all I've got. I can't bring back the years I've wasted, but I can be a better father to you in the time I have left."

Francie stood up. "I'll take Julien to the nursery, Char. Then I'm going to call Elliott." She took the sleeping baby in her arms and walked over to my chair, standing beside me. "Don't do it for us, Papa. Do it for Mamma." Her voice cracked. "For once in your life, *honor her.*"

Francie spun away, walking swiftly back to the house. With a lump in my throat, I watched her go, knowing she was bawling her eyes out. Her resentment toward Papa's treatment of Mamma surpassed mine, but I knew she'd grown up watching Mamma struggle each day just to breathe. Francie stood by whenever Papa showed up, helplessly watching as he looked for something to pawn, raiding the house of everything that wasn't nailed down. It was difficult, if not impossible, to believe anything he said, and her words indicated she wasn't ready to trust him. But then, neither was I.

Lillian appeared on the terrace and rushed down the wide, stone stairway. "My Lady," she said breathlessly as she neared us. "Chet is holding a car at the gate. He says it's from a medical facility! Someone must be ill…"

Papa stood up. "That's for me. I'll get my wallet and be right back."

"The car is from a treatment clinic," Adrienne said after Papa left. "I used the telephone in the house to call them this morning. They had a bed available and said they'd send a car for him." Her eyes mirrored uncertainty. "It's a private facility. Floyd will have to pay for it."

I sighed. "If he's serious about drying out, I'll pay for it. The trouble is, I have no proof that he truly intends to go through with this. He's not reliable, Adrienne."

I turned to Lillian. "Tell Chet to let the vehicle in." She returned to the house to relay the message.

"It's not by choice," Adrienne said. "We had a long talk last night. You know how direct I can be. I didn't mince words with him, nor did he with me."

That got my attention. "Really? What did you say?"

"What *I* said isn't important. What he told me was that a week ago he was drinking in a speakeasy and collapsed on the floor right in front of his cronies. He ended up in Ancker Memorial Hospital. The doctors told him he'd had a small heart attack and that his chance of having a massive one in the near future was likely."

I shrugged. "It had to come to that eventually. I'm surprised he's lasted this long."

She glanced back at the cottage. "He's afraid he's going to end up confined to a bed in an old folks' home."

I almost laughed at Papa's sudden concern about his health, but I kept my cynicism to myself. It was just like him to find himself at death's door before he decided to quit drinking. Whether he actually would go through with it was anybody's guess.

Will appeared on the terrace, motioning for us to join him.

Papa emerged from the cottage munching on a cookie. We went into the house and found the car waiting for him inside the carriage porch. Papa kissed me goodbye and got in the car.

I briefly filled Will in on the details.

"It's not a moment too soon," he said. "I wish him well."

"We'll see," I countered dubiously. Experience had taught me to refrain from getting my hopes up.

I turned to Adrienne as the car pulled away. "Come into the house. I've got a little surprise for you."

She and I went through the library into my office in the den. I walked behind my desk and pulled out the bottom drawer. Grabbing the bottle of expensive French wine, I set it on the desk, noticing the ribbon and tag had come untied and were still in the drawer. "This was in the closet." I gestured toward the door next to the bookcase. "I think it was intended for you."

"Oh?" Adrienne stood on the other side of the desk and frowned as she picked up the dark-colored bottle. "Why do you say that?"

"I think it goes with this." Reaching down into the drawer, I quickly tied the ribbon with the tag around the largest bundle of cash. "I found them together in a box." Straightening, I held out the bundle.

She gasped as she examined it in her hand. "What—how—I don't understand."

I stared innocently at the currency. "It appears to be a gift that Gus had intended to give you but never got the chance." I pointed to the tag. "That's his handwriting."

Adrienne's face flushed. "This is your money now. I can't take it."

"Why not? It's probably bootlegging profits that Gus would have spent on something else anyway—possibly another woman—so don't feel guilty about accepting it." I pushed her hand clutching the money toward her. "Consider it his way of posthumously making restitution for destroying your career."

"This—" She stared with amazement at the three-inch stack of twenty-dollar bills bound with a brown rubber band. "This is a lot of money."

"That it is." I smiled. "But then, we both know how generous Gus could be. Buy yourself a new wardrobe. Get your hair done. Enjoy it."

"It's been so long since I've had a new dress or a box of chocolates." Adrienne stared longingly at the cash. "I miss my Victrola, too. I used to have so many beautiful records."

I had no idea what had happened to her things but knew it would be rude to ask. "I think you should go shopping today."

Her dark eyes lit up with anticipation. "Would it be all right to ask Errol to give me a lift?"

"Of course. I expect him to take you wherever you want to go."

She checked her watch. "I'll go this afternoon if he has time."

The way she'd referred to the gardener so casually by his first name suggested she'd dropped in to chat with him on her nightly walk as well.

"That's a beautiful timepiece," I said, pointing at the platinum and diamond watch on her narrow wrist. "I've never seen you wear it before."

"I've always thought of it as an emergency fund. A way to get cash if I found myself in a bind." She stared at it wistfully. "Before I came here to stay, I was so desperate I nearly pawned it for money to live on. It was given to me by a former lover so I never wore it around Gus."

"Oh," I said, surprised by her admission. "The man certainly has good taste."

"Ralph Dixon has always had an eye for exquisite things." She looked up. "I used to sing in his nightclub. The one he had before he opened the Tansy Club. Gus saw me perform one night and stole me away from him."

Ralph Dixon? I stared at the watch, remembering how repulsive I'd found him the night I met him at the Tansy club. I recalled how he'd made a point of addressing me as *Mrs. LeDoux*. Thinking back to that night and the touch of his fingers grazing my shoulder gave me a sick feeling in the pit of my stomach.

"I must be going," Adrienne said and grabbed the bottle of wine. "I have to speak with Errol and get ready to go."

I pushed the troubling thoughts of Ralph Dixon from my mind.

"Absolutely! Enjoy your shopping trip!"

After Adrienne left the den, I sat down at my desk and smiled to myself, elated at how I'd used a simple bottle of wine to give her that gift of money. She urgently needed it but would have never accepted it otherwise.

With that accomplished, I went into the sunroom to lie down and listen to the radio. I'd barely pulled the blanket over my lap when Gerard appeared at the door. "You have a telephone call, My Lady."

It was Sally Wentworth and she was madder than a wet hen. "We've got more trouble at Anna's House, Charlotte!"

Oh, no. "What happened? Did you have another break-in?"

"Someone has been threatening the workers! Telling them to quit the job or risk getting beat up!"

It didn't take a genius to know who was behind the threats. I had suspected Leonard of orchestrating the break-in and the damage done to the interior of the building to delay the opening, but this little stunt unmistakably had his signature all over it.

"We need to ramp up our security," Sally said. "The house is set to open in a week and we're way behind schedule as it is. If our workers leave, we'll have to postpone it indefinitely."

"That won't be necessary," I said. "I'll take care of it."

I hung up, seething with anger at the interference I'd been contending with because I wouldn't do a deal with Leonard Murtagh. I wandered around the house for a while, mulling over the situation then called Harv and talked to him at length about a strategy to protect the workers so the house could open on time. We still had the grand opening to get through and we expected Leonard to try to sabotage it.

This time, however, we had a plan. We were one step ahead of him.

Chapter Fourteen

Mid-May

Harv held up his champagne flute. "I propose a toast to Anna's House in honor of your mother."

Riding in the Rolls Royce with the brothers, I held up my flute and shared a toast to my new adventure. Harv had opened a bottle of champagne to celebrate on the way to the grand opening. He and Marv were drinking the sparkling liquid. My glass was filled with ginger ale.

Marv returned from his trip yesterday. He was trying to give up cigarettes to please his Seattle sweetheart and had started chewing on Wrigley's Doublemint gum instead. The methodical smacking inside his cheek became annoying right away, but I had to admit, it was better than dodging a constant stream of smoke.

I'd insisted everyone, including Adrienne and Francie, come to the grand opening festivities of Anna's House. Both women had gone shopping and were wearing new dresses. I had on a light green dress made of silk canton crepe. The long-sleeved garment was low-waisted with a double-layered flared skirt. The collared front had a long, V-necked panel bordered with colorful embroidery and a necklace adorned with a large green tassel. I'd matched the dress with a green and white cloche hat, drop earrings, and my favorite French heels.

Harv topped off my soda. "When we get to the grand opening, I want you to take extra care to stay with Will and Dan. Do what they tell you, honey, so I don't have to worry about you."

"I will, Harv." I nodded obediently. "I promise."

Since my initial telephone call, Harv and I had engaged in several discussions surrounding the event. I'd assured Harv that Sally Wentworth had total control of the itinerary. My only job was to be there, hand her another envelope of cash and glad-hand the politicians who showed up. I'd used the rest of the bundles I'd found in Gus' safe in the den as my last donation for the construction so I didn't have to go to the bank again. After my last visit, I didn't want to approach Will about it. He and I had little to say to one another now, a change that deeply saddened me.

Harv had arranged extra bodyguards and additional cars to transport us all to the event. I'd insisted on riding with him and Marv so we could talk freely.

"There's something I need to tell you both," I said, staring into my flute. "It's been on my mind for a while."

The atmosphere in the Rolls suddenly changed. Both men looked at me with curiosity, as though they knew what I had planned to say. It made me even more nervous.

"Um..." I said, not knowing how to start the conversation. I only knew I had to tell them before Leonard decided to make it public.

"We've heard rumors about you and Will," Marv said cautiously. "Is there an announcement forthcoming?"

What? I grimaced. *My servants were probably the source of that...*

"No, not at all," I insisted, vigorously shaking my head. "This is about Gus."

Again, they went silent. More curious looks.

"The day Gus died," I began. "I..." I glanced from Harv to Marv.

"The truth is—he wasn't killed by a Federal agent. *I* shot him."

The brothers exchanged incredulous looks. "No, you didn't," Harv said with a disbelieving laugh. "Where did you get that idea?"

"When we were in the alley, Gus started to choke me and I grabbed the gun from his shoulder holster. I shot him and he went down." I glanced back and forth between the men, getting frustrated at their refusal to accept my confession. "I'm not making this up. I saw the blood. I killed him!"

"Wait," Harv said, adjusting his glasses, "are you talking about that injury to his side?"

"Yes! I'm responsible for that and it's been eating away at me ever since." I swallowed hard. "I never meant to hurt him. I just wanted him to stop hurting me."

Harv set down his flute. "That was merely a graze. It didn't kill him."

"But I saw him fall to the ground!"

"The shock probably knocked him out for a bit. A big guy like Gus wouldn't have been down very long. Then what happened?"

"Will found me kneeling over Gus. He carried me to a safe place. I didn't see what happened after that."

"Char, honey," Harv took my hand, looking gravely into my eyes, "that shot bled like crazy, but it didn't take him out. Gus' chest had been pumped full of lead. He was killed by someone with a Tommy gun."

I never knew this because Harv had claimed Gus' body at the morgue and took care of the funeral arrangements for me. "Why didn't you tell me this before?"

"We thought you knew," Marv said. "It was all over the newspapers."

"I purposely avoided reading them." I stared at my empty flute. "I

153

couldn't bear to see the gruesome pictures of Gus lying dead in a pool of blood." I looked up. "I didn't want to remember him that way."

Something wasn't right. Who would have killed a man that was already injured? Federal agents would have taken Gus to the hospital to keep him alive so they could put him on trial.

Only an enemy would have done that...

Leonard Murtagh had been Gus' bodyguard and driver. The one person who was supposed to meet us there. He must have come into the alley and seen me struggling with Gus. That's how Leonard knew I'd shot Gus. But why would Leonard kill him?

To be the next Gus LeDoux.

No wonder Leonard tried to frighten me by hinting at what he saw. When it didn't work, he'd sent the note.

Well, no more, I thought to myself as I stared at Harv. Today was the day to get my revenge. I just hoped it went according to our plan.

*　　*　　*

We arrived at Anna's House early, only to find the parking lot already full. I had no idea so many people cared about this endeavor! That said, Sally Wentworth had probably invited everyone who was anyone in St. Paul.

Harv and Marv walked me into the lobby, surrounded by a small army of suit-clad bodyguards, and escorted me into the ballroom, now referred to as the main hall. I gazed across the cavernous room, amazed at how much the place had changed. Sally's crew had left the stage and dance floor intact, but the rest of the room had been cleaned out. Rows of folding chairs had been arranged in front of the stage for the festivities. Along the wall in the back of the room, banquet tables covered in white linen had been set up, filled with an array of food and beverages. The rest of the hall was filled with round banquet tables where people sat talking and enjoying their appetizers. A special table had been set up in the corner with a huge cake that the baker had designed to look exactly like the building.

Sally Wentworth sat off to one side, giving an interview to a local reporter. The buxom redhead smiled profusely in her crisp, gray suit as a photographer snapped pictures of her. Good; I wanted Sally to get all the credit. She'd worked hard on this project and she deserved it.

The main hall was filling up quickly. We had a reserved spot near the stage, but Francie and Adrienne wanted to take a table in the back of the room. That was fine with me. I wanted to be able to leave quickly if needed without attracting attention. We sat down, sipping on strawberry punch, and munching on appetizers. Will and Daniel spaced themselves along the perimeter of the room, keeping watch over the crowd.

"This place is huge," Francie exclaimed, wide-eyed, as she nibbled on a cracker topped with a small square of cheese. "I wish I could have seen it when it was La Coquette." She stared wistfully at the stage. "I'll bet it was fun to come here on a Friday night and dance."

Adrienne sipped her punch, her scarlet lips leaving a waxy tattoo of lipstick on her paper cup. "I used to love the all-night dance competitions. People had so much fun." She glanced around. "This place holds many memories for me." She sighed. "Some good, some sad…"

After her interview, Sally came to see me. She approached our table with her arms outstretched. "Char! I'm so glad to see you!" She gave me a bear hug and then whispered in my ear, "You look a little peaked. Is everything all right?"

"Everything is fine," I whispered back. "I guess I haven't been myself since Mamma passed away." *And my doomed-to-fail relationship ended with Will.*

"I'm so sorry for your loss. My thoughts are with you and your sister as well." She hugged me, expressing her sympathy then made a grand sweep of her arm. "What do you think of the place? Would you like a tour?"

"You've done an amazing job." I smiled, relieved at the change of subject. "Yes, I'd love to see it!"

Sally instructed a passing waiter to place a reserved sign on our table. Then, with Will and Daniel trailing closely behind, she took Adrienne, Francie, and me through the layout of the facility. Sally had decided to keep Gus' office intact and designate it as the organization's office. I debated whether or not to tell her about the secret hideaway but decided to leave that for another time.

After we finished our tour and returned to the main hall, Adrienne and Francie went to the refreshment table for more punch. Sally took me aside. "I'm amazed at how friendly you've become with Gus' former mistress," she said boldly. "I'm afraid I couldn't be so forgiving."

"I've made peace with her and have tried to help her get back on her feet." I turned my back to the crowd and spoke in a low voice to avoid anyone overhearing our conversation. "She means me no harm."

Changing the subject to something more pleasant, I opened my purse and pulled out a thick envelope. "Here's the last installment of what I promised you for the renovation and the add-on of additional security costs."

Sally thanked me for the money and then left me to greet a dignitary that had just arrived. I headed downstairs to the ladies' room with my chaperones in tow. At the bottom of the stairs, Leonard Murtagh suddenly stepped out of the shadows, boldly confronting me. His posse stood behind him.

Will moved close, his arm outstretched in front of me, barring me from moving forward. Daniel was on my other side, his gun cocked.

"Out of the way, Murtagh," Will bellowed. "Let her pass!"

Leonard didn't move. He stood in the center of the hallway surrounded by his bodyguards. My heart pounded erratically at the sight of his gun leveled at my chest.

"What are you doing here," I said, forcing myself to speak in an annoyed voice. He must have snuck in through the service entrance. With all the caterers moving supplies and equipment in and out, no one would have noticed.

He regarded me with a mirthless grin. "So, you turned the building over to a charity because you didn't like my offer, eh?"

"Who told you that?" As if I cared...

"I've got a better one for you," Leonard said, ignoring my question. His grin spread wider. "Come closer and we'll talk."

"You're not going anywhere," Will said to me as he pointed his gun at Leonard.

"I'm worried that if I don't talk to him, he'll start trouble and ruin this event," I whispered.

Will didn't budge. "I said, you're not going anywhere, Charlotte and that's an *order*."

"Stars and Stripes Forever" played by a live orchestra began to echo down the stairway signaling the mayor's arrival. Leonard's bodyguards began to get restless.

"The Tansy Club," Leonard said quickly. "Dixon needs a lot of cash to get it back into shape so he can reopen it. I've talked to him about you. Told him we could do a three-way deal."

The mention of Ralph Dixon sent a chill down my spine. "Absolutely not! You double-crossed my husband," I said angrily. "*You* killed him—because you want to *be* him, but you'll never fill Gus' shoes. I wouldn't do a deal with you if you were the last man on earth. Get out and don't ever bother me again."

"You think you're immune to retaliation because you're Harv Katzenbaum's little darling?" Leonard's lips widened in an evil smile. "Your days are numbered, Char."

My heart hammered in my ears. The thought of getting shot and leaving my son an orphan frightened me so I could barely breathe.

"Pull that trigger and you won't get out of here alive," Daniel said in a guttural voice.

The heavy footsteps of Harv's men pounded on the stairway behind us.

Leonard and his associates quickly retreated, heading back to the service door to slip out of the building.

I desperately wanted to find Harv, but I knew Will wouldn't allow it. Instead, I went back upstairs with him and Daniel to join the party and wait for news about the scene I suspected was unfolding outside. As soon as I returned to my table, I scanned the hall looking for Harv, but he was nowhere to be found. Disappointed, I sat down and tried to listen to the Mayor's speech as I waited for Harv to appear. I was so keyed up that I couldn't concentrate. Eventually, I stood up, anxious to look for him.

Will grabbed my arm. "You're not going anywhere. Sit down."

I sat down, my stomach churning with anguish. I needed to know what was happening outside with Harv and Leonard. I was worried about Harv.

Suddenly, Harv appeared in the wide doorway of the lobby, his face grim. I waved at him until I caught his eye. He discreetly motioned for me to come to him. I stood up again, but this time Will didn't object. He took me by the arm and walked me around the back of the room. We reached the doorway and slipped into the lobby.

"What's going on?" I whispered in Harv's ear. "Did they catch Leonard?"

"See for yourself." He motioned to me to follow him to the front door and opened it an inch.

I peered through the crack as my heart fluttered. Two dozen

Federal agents were spread out in a wide circle, creating a human chain while other men were directing a paddy wagon as it backed toward the building. Leonard and his men lay face down on the ground, their hands handcuffed behind their backs. Harv had gotten revenge for Gus without firing a single shot.

Harv stood behind me and stared at the incident over the top of my head. "Somebody gave an anonymous tip to the Feds that Leonard might show up to disrupt the grand opening. With all the politicians and fat cats in attendance, I guess they took it seriously."

Leonard had snuck out of the building and into the trap set by the Feds. All while the Mayor was giving his speech to a packed room of politicians and wealthy patrons. I had no doubt the scene would be cleared by the time the event ended.

"I hope that arrest sticks," I whispered, worrying that if Leonard got out on bail, he might come after me again.

"He's going up the river for the rest of his life," Harv said smugly. "He killed a couple of Federal agents the night La Coquette was raided."

I breathed a sigh of relief. No more bodyguards. No more lockdown. My family was safe and I was free to go on with my life. Sadly, without Will.

*   *   *

The next morning, Gerard stood at the door to my office in the den. "My Lady, you must come at once. Miss Francie is out on the terrace with Miss Adrienne."

The urgency in his usually deadpan voice prompted me to spring from my chair and follow him through the house. Out on the terrace, Francie and Adrienne sat together on a padded bench. Francie held a large, balled-up handkerchief in her hands as she cried her eyes out while Adrienne tried to comfort her.

I rushed toward them. "What's wrong?"

Francie looked up; fresh tears streaking her red, puffy face. "I hate him! He's a coward!"

Dragging a chair over to her, I sat down and took her hands in mine. "Who is a coward?"

"Elliott!"

Okay...

Adrienne and I exchanged knowing glances.

"What happened?"

Francie dabbed at her eyes. "Elliott lied to me. He told me he cared for me—more than any girl he'd ever known. Then all of a sudden, he started to ignore me. I've been calling him for three days and leaving messages but he wouldn't call me back. Today, his aunt told me Elliott wasn't going to be home until later." She burst into a loud sob. "She said he had taken his girlfriend to a matinee at the cinema!"

Thank you, Leon. I breathed a silent sigh of relief, glad to be rid of that sneaky kid for good.

"From now on," Francie said with a hiccup, "I'm going to be just like you, Char! Men are going to chase *me*, not the other way around."

Adrienne and I exchanged glances again. I may have appeared to be a tough woman to my sister, but deep inside, my heart ached over a man who had rejected me. I must have done a better job of covering it up than I'd realized.

"If you want to be like me," I said in a solemn tone, "then get serious about your studies and bring up your grades. I married Gus in tenth grade, but I continued to go to school until I graduated." I leaned forward. "Don't expect a man to define who you are or make you happy. You need to find happiness within yourself. Only then can you be happy with someone else."

My sister stared at me, wide-eyed, taking in my words, but I meant them as an encouragement to myself as well.

*   *   *

Later that morning, I stood in the center of Gus' walk-in closet, pondering the job of removing his clothing. I'd decided to move into his room and make it my own. It was twice the size of mine and had a nice-sized closet. Besides, after that serious discussion I'd had with Francie, I realized it was high time I got on with my *own* life as well.

I planned to box up everything and give it to charity. Lillian had offered to help me sort through the items, but I insisted on doing that part myself. I wanted to go through the pockets of each piece of clothing as I pulled it out of the closet to make sure Gus hadn't left anything of value in it. Or any secrets…

I spent an hour cleaning his dresser and found a few bundles of cash plus some gold cufflinks I'd given him for Christmas but nothing else of value. I gathered up his shoes, ties, underwear, and hats, setting everything on the bed for Lillian to place into boxes. Then I went through his suits, one by one, and piled them on the bed, which by now was heaped with his clothing.

Lillian entered the bedroom with a stack of empty wooden fruit crates. "Is there anything to clean out in the closet of Gus' study?"

Her question gave me pause. "I don't know. I'll check."

I went into his study and opened the closet door. I hadn't looked in there in years because I expected it to be empty. It was just as I anticipated—empty—but there was something *odd* about it that caught my eye. All of the bedrooms on this floor had closets with lighting and wood flooring, but the walls were plain. The walls in this closet had wainscoting on them. Ornately carved wainscoting, like in the dining room downstairs.

"What in the world…" I said aloud, looking around. "When did he have this installed? And why did he go to all the trouble to make it look like the walls in the dining room?" It didn't make sense to put so much work into a room he'd never intended to use. I stood there for a minute looking at the walls and wondering what Gus' frame of mind had been when he'd had this closet remodeled. The paneling even had the exact design as—

Suspicious, I slipped out of my shoes and got down on my knees to get a better look at the wood, examining every inch. In the center of the fourth panel, I saw it; the metal button. Like the one in the dining room for the silver vault. I placed my finger on it and suddenly began to sweat, wondering what would happen when I pushed it.

Click.

The panel opened up, and behind it, I found a combination lock on a large door. Swallowing hard, I stared at it, wondering what was behind it. I spun the dial, using the combination to the silver vault, but came up short. That wasn't the right set of numbers.

I shut the panel and went into the study, pulling everything apart, looking for the information. After fifteen minutes of exhaustive searching, I stood back, frustrated, staring at the room. Where could Gus have hidden that combination? Perhaps he'd simply memorized it and never intended to write it down.

Letting out a deep breath, I walked into the hallway, contemplating my options. I could hire someone to crack the code for me—

"No, no," I said to myself as I paced the hallway. "There is something behind that door he didn't want anyone to see. Otherwise, he would have put it in the safe in the den…"

I froze. *Perhaps both of them have the same combination.*

Lillian came into the hallway. "Did you say something, My Lady?"

"Ah…I need to go downstairs for a minute. I'll be right back," I yelled as I flew down the stairway. I ran across the hall, through the library, and into the den where I pulled the sliding ladder over to the spot where Harv had pulled out the book.

Five minutes later, I was still looking through the books on the top shelf, desperately trying to figure out which one had the combination written in it. I'd put the book back myself so why couldn't I find it now?

Think...see it in your mind.

It was blue, clothbound and I'd put it back with my right hand... That was when Will had appeared in the doorway and I'd become so distracted, I'd lost track of what I was doing.

I looked up, pulled out all of the blue books, and checked them. One was upside down. I turned it right side up and checked the front flap. There it was! Laughing with relief, I climbed down the ladder, promising myself I'd write that combination down in another place that I could easily access.

I ran upstairs and burst into Gus' study, shutting the door behind me. As I entered the closet, I shut that door as well. *Well, here goes...* Within seconds, I was back to where I left off, working the dial with one hand, and reading the numbers in the book.

Something clicked. This one sounded different—solid. I turned the handle and pulled on the door. It opened. I blinked as I stared into a dark cavern. This was no vault. It was a storage space. My fingers traveled up and down the inside wall, looking for a light switch. When I found it, I turned on the light and in slow motion, my jaw dropped.

It was a secret room.

In total awe, I slowly absorbed the magnitude of the windowless chamber. It wasn't a big area, maybe eight feet by ten feet, but guns of every size and brand hung on the outside wall. Boxes of ammunition were stacked on a long, waist-high bookshelf on the floor that stretched from corner to corner. Several large ledgers were stored on the bottom shelf of the bookcase. The remainder of the room was furnished with a small sofa, a drum table with a Tiffany lamp, a large steamer trunk, and a coffee table made of inlaid walnut positioned in front of the sofa. Like the secret room I'd found at Anna's House, the entire floor was covered with a thick rug.

This is Gus' hideout. Another safe haven from his enemies. My late husband had been either very paranoid or very cunning.

An opened pack of cigarettes, a glass ashtray, and a small wooden box of matches were on the coffee table. Next to that, I observed a bottle of whiskey, partially consumed, and a crystal lowball glass. I stared at the items as a sense of Gus' presence overwhelmed me. I shook it off and turned to leave when my foot struck something solid under the coffee table. Curious, I bent down to see what it was and gasped. The two-foot by three-foot table didn't have legs. The tabletop was sitting upon a solid block of bundled currency. The block stretched the entire width and length of the tabletop and stood probably two feet high. I had always believed that Gus laundered his bootlegging money through his businesses but I was wrong. He'd stored it here. All of it.

Oh, my gosh...

Suddenly, I knew what was in the steamer trunk. I stepped toward it and lifted the lid. It was filled to the brim with money. Counted, banded, and tightly stacked. So, this was what Leonard was looking for when he broke into my soda shops. Or at least, some clue as to its whereabouts.

Dazed, I walked out of the room and switched off the light. I shut the door and pressed the button to move the panel back into place. I doubted anyone would believe me if I told them about Gus' hidey-hole—or the money. On the other hand, even if I wanted to tell someone, confiding in the wrong person could jeopardize my security. And my life.

This was one secret belonging to Gus that I decided to keep all to myself.

Chapter Fifteen

That evening...

Gazing through the glass jewelry case, I saw so many beautiful pieces, I couldn't make up my mind which one I liked best. I pointed toward a diamond bracelet. "What do you think of this one, Harv?"

Harv peered down into the case. "Very nice. You pick out whatever you want, honey. Your golden birthday only comes once in a lifetime."

My twenty-sixth birthday had actually occurred in late April, around the time I received that unsigned, threatening note and couldn't go out to celebrate. Harv hadn't forgotten, though, and promised I could have whatever I wanted today.

The jeweler, an older man with gray hair parted down the center and wearing tortoiseshell glasses, retrieved his heavy ring of keys on a chain fastened to his belt loop and unlocked the case. "Would you like to try it on?"

I stared at the pretty string of diamonds set in white gold. "Yes, please."

He reached into the case and took out the black velvet display pad. "This tennis bracelet is a beautiful specimen of two different cuts—the round brilliant cut, and the rectangular baguette."

I held out my hand and watched as he carefully placed the bracelet on my wrist. It fit perfectly. I lifted my wrist to the light. The diamonds sparkled with dazzling brilliance. I nodded. "I love it. I'll take this one."

The jeweler smiled. "Would you like me to put it in a box for you, Miss, or would you rather wear it?"

"Oh, I'm going to wear it," I replied emphatically. I thanked each of the brothers with a kiss on the cheek for my special gift.

Marv pulled a long, flat wallet from the inside of his jacket and paid the man in cash while Harv escorted me back to the Rolls Royce. Once we were settled, he handed me a Champagne flute. "Are you sure you don't want any wine?"

I shook my head. "Lately, I haven't had much desire for liquor. I'll stick with ginger ale."

I'd lost interest in drinking ever since the night I drank too much with Will, but I kept that information to myself. Every time I thought about that night and what happened when I came back from my trip up north, a cloud of sadness descended over me.

Once Marv emerged from the jewelry store and joined us in the Rolls, we were off to Harv's victory dinner. With Leonard out of the way, his territory had not only been saved, but he was expanding it to include Leonard's suppliers as well. Harv wanted to celebrate at the newest hotspot in St. Paul, an Italian restaurant on West Seventh Street called Tresanti's, a few blocks down from my Ford dealership. It had been so long since I'd been out for an evening on the town that I looked forward to it with great anticipation. My mouth watered at the thought of crusty garlic bread and a plate of cheesy lasagna.

The chauffeur dropped us off at the curb and we walked up the wide sidewalk to the front entrance, a small room where people waited for their transportation. Inside the entrance, the aromas of spicy sausage and garlic filled the air. The building shook from foot stomping and hand clapping to lively Italian music. We went through another door to the lobby.

Harv approached the host stand. "The Katzenbaum party at seven o'clock."

The host, clad in a white shirt, dark trousers, and a floor-length apron, nodded to Harv. "Yes, sir. Right this way please." He led us through the busy restaurant to a large round table in the corner.

Francie, Adrienne, Will, and Daniel were already seated. I had requested Adrienne and Francie be invited as well and Harv agreed. Will and Daniel had escorted them. Harv pulled out the empty chair next to Will and motioned for me to sit. I sat down with Will on my right and Harv on my left.

Right away, Francie noticed the bracelet on my wrist and asked where I'd gotten it. I held out my hand for everyone to see what the brothers had given me for my birthday. Francie ogled it and wasted no time in asking me if she could wear it sometime. I smiled but didn't give her an answer. I had already planned to buy her a pretty bracelet like mine for Christmas.

Harv pulled a bottle of wine from a leather pouch and discreetly handed it off to our waiter. The wine was served and Harv initiated a toast for my birthday. Francie and I had ginger ale.

Appetizers were next. While we ate, an older, heavyset man playing the accordion came around to our table and played a special song for me. Then he played one for Francie and one for Adrienne. We clapped and sang along.

Everyone appeared to be having a good time except for Will. He seemed preoccupied but I was used to that. As my bodyguard, he never let his guard down, especially when we went out in public.

I leaned close to get his attention. "Adrienne and Daniel seem to be hitting it off quite well, don't you think? He's nonstop with the teasing and funny stories. She can't stop laughing."

Will glanced their way but didn't smile at their obvious attraction to each other. "Yeah, he's been volunteering to patrol the grounds a lot lately. He likes the way she sings all the time in her cottage with the windows open."

A waiter took away my appetizer plate and set a soup bowl in front of me. A large tureen filled with minestrone sat in the center of the table. In this restaurant, the meals were served family-style.

"She came into some money and bought herself a new Victrola," I said casually. "She's trying to get her voice back into shape to sing professionally again."

"If I'd known that, I would have given her mine," Will replied.

Harv took the cover off the tureen and spooned the soup into our bowls.

I picked up my spoon. "You have a beautiful Victrola. Why would you want to give it away?"

"I don't have much use for it anymore."

His answer bothered me. As his former housekeeper, I'd spent many Saturdays preparing wonderful food for his dinner parties. What had happened to all the friends he used to entertain? "What about all of the parties you used to have at your house?"

He shrugged. "Too busy working."

I fell silent and ate my soup. Marv made a silly joke and I struggled to laugh. Will didn't find it funny either and I placed my hand upon his to ask what was wrong. Before I had a chance to speak, he pulled his hand away.

The waiter removed the tureen and replaced it with platters of salad and garlic bread. I took a piece of warm, crusty bread and turned to pass the platter to Will when Adrienne caught my eye. She sat deathly still; her face flushing with fear as she stared at something in the distance. I glanced around to see what had frightened her and almost dropped the plate. On the other side of the room, Ralph Dixon sat at a large round table with his wife and family, his piercing gaze fixed upon Adrienne. Then it shifted toward me. I flinched at the vengeful stare in his cold dark eyes.

"What's wrong?" Will's hand automatically slipped inside his coat.

"Oh, nothing serious. This plate holding the garlic bread is hot," I answered quickly and passed it to him. In my head, a different set of words churned—

Just a man staring venomously at the woman the late Gus LeDoux stole from him. And the widow who forgave them both.

When the next course was served, Harv passed a large bowl of ravioli to me. I selected only two of the pillow-shaped pasta covered in red sauce and set them on my plate. I was already so full I couldn't eat much more but I needed to save room for coffee and dessert.

"Ravioli?" I passed the bowl to Will, pressing my shoulder against his.

"Harv and I had a discussion this morning," Will said solemnly as he grasped the bowl and shifted his arm away from me. "Now that Murtagh and his gang are in jail without bail, Dan and I have finished our assignment. I'd planned to tell you later, but it's getting so late, I figured I wouldn't get the chance. We'll be leaving early tomorrow morning."

His words crushed my heart. "Already? Are you sure?"

Will spooned a pile of ravioli onto his plate. "If you have issues with our assessment of the situation, I suggest you take it up with Harv. He's indicated to me that he thinks you need to have a permanent set of bodyguards, but that's between you and him."

Now that Leonard was incarcerated, I had no intention of hiring permanent bodyguards, but I didn't say so. I didn't want to start an argument with him during his last night on the job.

"This is all so sudden," I said instead, making my frustration obvious.

"The arrangement Harv made with me was only temporary," Will replied. "Dan and I have to get back to our own business. Peter's getting anxious. He's got a lot of cases piling up that he needs to be investigated and he'd rather not hire another firm to handle them."

I remembered Peter Garrett well, the attorney who shared an office with Will and Daniel. The pair handled all of Peter's investigative work. He was also engaged to Will's sister, Madeline.

Will dived into his dinner, leaving me to silently process the disappointing news.

By the time dessert arrived, I was so stuffed I couldn't move, but I ended up sharing a piece of warm chocolate cake with a scoop of vanilla ice cream with Francie.

It was after nine o'clock by the time we stood up to leave and the restaurant was nearly empty. Daniel went out ahead of us to inform Harv's chauffeur and bodyguards to bring the car around to the front.

Harv and Marv went out first to meet up with their bodyguards. Will and Daniel followed; Adrienne, Francie, and I were last. As soon as he gave me the signal, I ventured outside and breathed in the fresh night air. Straight ahead, several cars were parked at the curb. Our chauffeur stood at the open door of the Rolls, waiting for us to board. As I emerged from the building, a black car suddenly came out of nowhere. It took a quick left turn and screeched to a stop in the driveway of the restaurant parking lot. A half-dozen men jumped out—with guns blazing.

"Char!" Will's arm pressed against me, pushing me back inside the entrance. "Get down!"

I fell back against Adrienne and Francie taking them both down with me. My heart pounded in fear as we lay on the floor, covering our ears with our hands and screaming at the warfare taking place outside. Torrents of bullets exploded outside the entrance. Some ricocheted over our heads, smashing the windows and showering us with glass. What seemed like an eternity lasted probably less than a minute. When the firing stopped, the atmosphere held an air of deadly calm.

The door burst open and Harv stared down at us, his hands covered in blood. "Ladies! Are you okay?"

Ignoring his question, we bombarded him with a barrage of our own hysterical inquiries. Satisfied that we were all right, he stepped away and let the door slam shut.

Gingerly, I crawled to the doorway and pushed it open. The hazy air reeked with the acrid odor of gunpowder, burning my throat and eyes. Motionless bodies lay strewn across the ground. Daniel crouched behind the open door of the Rolls pointing his gun at the bullet-riddled car of our attackers in the driveway as though he expected more gunfire to erupt from it. Harv kneeled over Marv, examining his bleeding shoulder. He saw me and his eyes narrowed. "Char! Get back inside!" The stark ruthlessness in his voice startled me. I'd never seen this side of him before. It reminded me of Gus' reaction the day La Coquette was raided. "Do it now!" He turned toward Daniel. "Get an ambulance!"

Daniel glanced around furtively as he ran toward me, still tightly clutching his gun. He was alone. "Char, do as Harv says!"

"Where's Will?" I screamed as I frantically searched the area. Then I saw him, lying on his back on the ground, blood oozing from his mid-section.

"Will!" Disregarding caution, I crawled over to him and leaned over his body, sobbing. "Will, can you hear me?"

Slowly, he opened his eyes. His face twisted with pain as he tried to speak.

"Don't try to talk. Please—you need to conserve your strength. Daniel just went into the restaurant to call an ambulance."

His lips kept moving. What was he trying to say? Was he lying on his gun or—

"What's the matter?" Seeing him in such great pain frightened me. I leaned over him, placing my ear close to his lips.

"If I don't make it..." he struggled to whisper, "I love you." The words were barely discernable, but to me, they were crystal clear.

I lifted my head and looked into his troubled eyes. "Oh, Will. I love you so much—"

His eyes closed.

Dear God, no.

"Will!" I screamed through my hysterical sobs. "Will! Don't leave me. Please don't leave me now!"

*　　*　　*

"Don't cry, Char. He's going to make it through this. He's going to be okay."

Daniel placed his arm around my shoulders and tried to comfort me with hopeful words as we sat in the hospital waiting room with a handful of strangers, all of us frantic with worry about the fates of our loved ones. Wiping my tears and smudged makeup on what used to be Daniel's snow-white cotton handkerchief, I anxiously waited for word of Will's condition. Daniel and I had been sitting in this depressing room with yellowed walls and a gray tiled floor for almost three hours. I still wore my blood-stained dress. My back ached from sitting on a hard, wooden chair. The place reeked with the stench of antiseptic and the lack of fresh air made it difficult to keep from losing my dinner.

My gaze clung to a large, round wall clock whose hands moved with glacial speed as we waited, noting that it was almost one o'clock in the morning and still no one had come to give us an update on what was happening to Will. Watching medical personnel pull other people out of the room to speak with them made me wonder if anyone knew I was waiting for news.

Desperately waiting.

The gunfight had taken the lives of all of the men who'd attacked us and four of Harv's men. His two remaining bodyguards were transported to the hospital by ambulance along with Marv and Will. I didn't have any idea what their conditions were, but Harv had dropped by the waiting room to give me a much-needed hug and find out about Will's condition. He gave me the good news that Marv would recuperate from his shoulder wound. His angry demeanor had faded, but I still sensed a tenseness in him I'd never experienced before.

The shooting had left my sister in hysterics. I'd tried my best to comfort her with hugs and assurances that she was safe now, but at the time I was in shock myself and could barely speak through my sobbing. Adrienne took control of Francie's situation immediately and arranged for the police to take them home, allowing me to accompany Will to the hospital.

"Will warned me," I said to Daniel, "about Harv. He said it would be impossible to be close to Harv without suffering the repercussions of his illegal activities." I sniffled into my handkerchief. "I didn't believe him."

Daniel gently squeezed my shoulders. "I don't know why it happened tonight, but the way it was done, no one could have predicted it."

"When Harv finds out who ambushed him, he'll retaliate." I looked into Daniel's green eyes. They reflected intelligence and wisdom. "I don't want to be a casualty of his war."

"Then do the right thing by yourself, Char," Daniel countered, sounding like the older brother I never had. "Harv helped you when you needed it, and you should be thankful to him for that, but it's time to go your own way. Establish new relationships with people who share your interests. Become Charlotte LeDoux in your own right instead of being known as Gus' widow."

My heart ached at the thought, but I knew it was time to let go of the brothers, the men who'd stepped into the role of the father I never had. Though I loved them both with all my heart, from now on I would love them from a distance. The clever capture of Leonard Murtagh showed me that Harv's cunning ways were making him more powerful than Gus. In time, he would become more ruthless than Gus was, too, because once a man muscled his way to the top of the gangster heap, that was the only way he could remain there. I didn't want to get caught up in that world again. It had driven a wedge between Will and me. Armed with what I knew now, I would move heaven and earth to hear him say "I love you" again.

A tall, slender woman appeared in the waiting room doorway in a bright red dress, scanning the crowd for someone. It had been six months since the last time I saw her, but she hadn't changed a bit. She still wore her black hair short and her dresses even shorter than most women dared to, unabashedly showing off her long, slender legs. I jumped out of my chair and ran to greet Will's only sibling. "Madeline!"

Madeline Van Elsberg met me in the center of the room and engulfed me with a tearful hug. "I'd have come sooner, but I was out for the evening and didn't get home until after midnight. The police were waiting for me and said that Will had been hospitalized, but they wouldn't give me any details. How is he?"

"I don't know. I've been waiting for nearly three hours and haven't received any news yet." I sniffled. "I'm exhausted."

She pulled away; her cheeks were wet with worry as she stepped back. Suddenly, she noticed the bloodstains on my dress. "Oh, my goodness, Charlotte. What happened?"

I took a deep breath. "We were ambushed coming out of a restaurant."

She ran her hands through her chin-length curls as her blue eyes flashed with worry. "I was afraid something like this might happen to Will someday. His profession is too dangerous!" She grabbed me by the hand and pulled me toward the door. "Come on, we're going to find someone to give us some information."

"We'll be back," I called to Daniel as we practically flew out of the room.

"Who's in charge?" Madeline demanded from the first hospital staff we encountered.

The young man in brown work clothes pointed down the corridor to a large desk. "The nurse's station is that way. I'm just the janitor."

Madeline pulled me down the hallway and confronted the nurse on duty. "Are you in charge here?"

The woman stood up. "I *am*," she answered in an authoritative voice. She wore a starched white apron over her light green dress and a white cap on her head. "I'm Nurse Ekstrom. What can I do for you?"

"I demand to know the condition of my brother!"

Nurse Ekstrom's stoic expression was unflappable. "His name?"

"William Van Elsberg," Madeline said. "He was admitted about three hours ago. I'm his sister, Madeline and this is his fiancée," she said, giving me a quick wink, "Charlotte LeDoux."

Nurse Ekstrom's tone softened a little. "Mr. Van Elsberg is still in surgery." She wrote Madeline's name on her patient chart and gestured toward the hallway. "I'll ask Doctor Samuelson when he comes out of surgery to speak with you in the waiting room, but I'm afraid I can't tell you what time that will be."

Disappointed, we went in search of a place to sit down where we could talk privately for a few minutes. We ended up in the hallway around the corner from the waiting room, sitting on a wooden bench. I gave Madeline a short rundown of what happened.

"I don't know if Will told you or not, but I broke my engagement to Peter," Madeline said seriously. Reaching down, she pulled a small silver flask from the garter that held up her stocking.

Shocked at the news, I placed my hand on her arm. "I'm so sorry, Maddie, that things didn't work out for you." Only Will and her closest friends called her Maddie.

Madeline shrugged. "It's for the best, I guess. Peter and I were never really suited to each other anyway." She sighed. "He's looking for an old-fashioned girl. Someone who wants to get married, settle down, and have a tribe of kids. Bake cakes and get fat." She laughed. "Me, I just want to have fun. Take life one day at a time."

I smiled inwardly. That was Madeline all right. The life of the party. The first time I met her she'd just come from a nightclub where she'd been making merry with her friends.

Madeline unscrewed the cap of her flask. "That's enough about my crazy life. How about you? How is the romance progressing with my brother? He's not very talkative about such things."

Downcast, I picked at a nail. "One day everything is going well and the next day, it isn't. He's sensitive about some things—I've learned that the hard way." I looked up. "Someone must have really stomped on his heart." *Worse than I did...*

Madeline nodded. "The gal's name was Eva. Will was dizzy in love with that dame and wanted to marry her but after they got engaged, she dumped him for a guy with a fancy car and a ticket to the big-time life in New York City." Madeline took another swig of liquor and grimaced as she swallowed it down. "As luck would have it, I introduced them."

I stood, anxious to get back to Daniel. "We should go back to the waiting room."

Madeline recapped her flask and slipped it back under her garter. "I'd rather go back and rattle that nurse's cage. She knows more than she's telling. I could sense it when we were talking to her."

Madeline opened her handbag and pulled out a tube of lipstick and a mirror. She dabbed her favorite shade of red-orange lipstick on her lips as we walked back into the waiting room. At this point, I didn't care what I looked like. I just wanted to know if Will was going to live.

I made a beeline to Daniel the moment we returned. "Any news?"

He frowned, his thick coppery mustache turning down at the corners of his mouth. "Not a thing."

By that time, only one other person remained in the waiting room, a man slumped in a chair with a newspaper covering his face. Nighttime in the hospital was eerily quiet. Madeline and I sat down next to Daniel and commenced to watch the clock.

"Miss Madeline Van Elsberg?"

The masculine voice startled me awake. I sat up in surprise and opened my heavy-lidded eyes. My head swam with dizziness.

Where am I?

"Doctor Samuelson?" Madeline sprang from her chair, reminding me we were in the hospital. She approached a young man standing in the doorway wearing a white coat. Getting my bearings, I stood up and stumbled, but Daniel took my arm and steadied me as we followed her.

"I'm Doctor Hedin," the young man responded. "Doctor Samuelson has gone home." I stood next to Madeline, clinging to her arm for support. "Mr. Van Elsberg's surgery was successful. He's a lucky man. The bullet missed his spine and Doctor Samuelson was able to remove it without damaging any of his internal organs."

177

"When can we see him?" Madeline and I both asked at the same time.

"He's in critical, but stable condition. You may see him now but limit your visit to a couple of minutes."

The doctor left us in the care of Nurse Ekstrom and the three of us followed her to the ward where Will was in a bed near the door. "There are other patients in this ward," she whispered, "so please be quiet."

Will lay unconscious, his face deathly pale against his dark hair. I clutched the side of the bed for support when I saw him. Madeline and I stood at his side. Daniel stood at the end of the bed, silently observing his partner. His face was stricken.

"Oh, Will," Madeline whispered as she broke down and covered her face with her hands. "Please don't die. You can't die. You're all I've got…"

The thought of Will never regaining consciousness shook me to the core. I couldn't accept spending the rest of my life without him.

No, he can't… I can't…

I was suddenly so hot I couldn't breathe. My knees gave way as I sunk to the floor. Then everything went black…

Chapter Sixteen

A day later...

I awoke, squinting against the sunlight streaming through my bedroom window. Only I wasn't in my room. I was in Gus' room. What was I doing here? I'd planned to move my things in here and sleep in here permanently but hadn't made the change yet.

Lillian stood next to the bed, pulling open the drapes.

Closing my eyes again, I stretched and yawned.

"Good morning, My Lady!" Lillian's chipper voice greeted me. "How are you feeling today?"

I rubbed my eyes. "Hungry. I feel like I haven't eaten in a week." My empty stomach was queasy.

She smiled profusely. "I'll tell Cook to prepare your breakfast immediately. Would you like coffee and juice right away?"

I nodded. "What time is it? I don't remember going to bed in here."

Lillian's face sobered. "It's Saturday morning. Daniel brought you home last night. He had to carry you into the house because you were so exhausted. Don't you remember? You fainted at the hospital."

Wha—what? Then I remembered why I had gone there with Daniel. *Will is in the hospital!*

I sat up quickly and threw off the covers. "Never mind breakfast. I have to get dressed! I have to go to the hospital and check on Will's condition!"

"You need to stay put for a while, My Lady, and have some strong coffee." She rang the service bell. "I'll be back with your coffee in a couple of minutes. Please, you must lie down and rest until I get back!"

She didn't need to ask again. The dizziness in my head was convincing enough. I lay back against the pillows knowing I'd have to take it easy for a little while before I got up again, but I *was* going to get up, get dressed, and go back to the hospital. If Daniel wasn't around, I'd ask Errol to escort me.

The last thing I remembered about Friday night was standing over Will's bed. Then…nothing. It must have been the stress of seeing him so ill—the deathly pallor of his face—that had caused me to pass out, but I was determined not to embarrass myself like that again.

Francie burst into the bedroom. "Lillian just told me you were awake. What happened at the hospital to make you faint? Did you see something really scary?" She climbed onto the bed and sat next to me. The first thing I noticed about her was that she had on my cultured pearl drop earrings and my blue georgette blouse. It irritated me, but I decided not to make a fuss over it.

"I saw Will after he came out of surgery." I rubbed my eyes with the heels of my hands. "Will's sister, Madeline, was there, too, and when she started crying because she thought he might die, that's when I fainted." I threw my arm across my eyes, determined not to cry in front of my sister. "It was just too much for me to take." Composing myself, I pulled my arm away and lifted my head off the pillow. "Has Maddie called? Have you heard anything about how he's doing?"

Francie shook her head. "She called early this morning to see how you were and said there was no change in Will's condition. So far, no one else has called." Her brows knitted together in concern. "There's something I need to tell you."

I sat up slowly, bracing myself with my hands. *Please, dear Lord, don't let it be anything to do with her and Elliott...* "What happened?"

"It's not *what* happened," she said, correcting me. "It's *why*."

My arms began to wobble, forcing me to recline again. "I don't understand what you mean."

She slid off the bed and peered into the other bedroom as if to make sure no one would overhear what she was about to say. "I heard the police talking among themselves last night. There were so many coppers at the scene of the shooting that a lot of them were just standing around." She climbed back onto the bed and sat with her feet dangling over the side. "Some of the coppers said the guys that shot at us were button men hired to kill the brothers." She shivered at her own words. "Some thought it was payback from Leonard's family for turning him into the Feds because he's going to prison for life, but others disagreed. They said it was about Gus."

"Gus?" I blinked. "That's ridiculous. He's been dead for almost ten months. How on earth could he be responsible for what happened?"

Francie frowned. "I heard them say there were bootleggers who envied Gus and when he died, there was a lot of anger about the brothers swooping in and taking over his business." She fiddled with one of her earrings. "I had a bad dream last night about the shooting. The brothers like you a lot, but I don't want us to go anywhere with them anymore, okay?" She gave me a frightened look. "I'm scared to be around them now."

Francie's remark shook me to the core.

"I'm sorry about what happened," I said softly. "I've been thinking about that, too. Harv never meant to put either of us at risk, but we can't associate with him any longer."

I should have known something like this would happen eventually.

Will had warned me that my friendship with Harv would pull me deeper and deeper into his world until something disastrous happened, but I didn't believe it. My heart ached at how I'd unknowingly placed my sister in harm's way.

"Don't worry, Francie." I sat up and hugged my sister to assure her I took her fears seriously. "I'm going to make sure we never go through that ever again. I promise."

There was only one way to ensure the safety of my family. I'd have to hire a team of bodyguards—the very thing I'd always been against. This time, though, the situation would be entirely different. I would hire them myself. They would work for *me*, be loyal to *me,* and take orders from *me.* Instead of making me feel like a prisoner in my own home, they would give me the freedom I longed for because for once in my life I had complete control of my destiny.

Lillian appeared in the doorway with my coffee and juice on a tray. I drank my coffee and visited with Francie until my breakfast came. She grabbed a piece of my toast and went to her room to wash her hair. Like an obedient child, I ate all of the food Cook had put on my tray. I didn't want to give anyone on my staff cause to worry about my health. By the time I'd finished, I felt much better. My stomach wasn't queasy any longer.

By two o'clock, I was ready to go out. I had spoken to Daniel about staying on as my bodyguard for a while longer and to my relief, he agreed. While Errol was bringing the car around to the front, I made a call to Harv to check on Marv. According to the housekeeper, Harv had left town on a business trip and she was quick to say she didn't know where he'd gone. Marv was recuperating fine but getting grumpier by the minute because he needed a drink and a cigarette—even though he was supposedly trying to quit smoking. Indulging in either habit was against the doctor's orders so Harv had forbidden anyone to give in to Marv's demands. I told her I was coming over to visit Marv, but not to tell him about it. I wanted to surprise him. I also wanted to leave a message for Harv.

After I checked on Marv, Daniel and I went straight to the hospital. We stopped at the nurse's station for an update on Will's condition and I found out he was doing better but still in a lot of pain. Worried, I went into his ward to see him. He was sleeping. I pulled a chair up to his bed and sat down. After a few minutes, Daniel left to get some fresh air and update Errol on Will's condition, but I knew he was also allowing me to have time alone with Will.

I sat quietly, watching him sleep, yearning to have the old Will back again; the man who used to tip his hat to me, the man who showed me how to drive and kiss at the same time. The man who taught me how to love again…

He groaned in pain.

I took his hand in mine. A lump formed in my throat. My eyes filled with tears as I began to quietly pray. The moment he heard my voice, he slowly opened his eyes. My heart fluttered with joy. "Will, it's me, Char. Are you in pain? Do you want me to get the nurse?"

He tried to speak to me but his lips could only form raspy sounds.

"It's okay," I whispered as I cupped his face in my hands. "Don't try to talk. Save your strength." His lips looked parched and I wondered if he needed a drink of water. I filled the glass from a pitcher on the metal table between the beds and placed the paper straw in his mouth so he could drink, hoping it would soothe his throat.

When he finished, I took the cup away. The pain in his eyes frightened me. "I'll get the nurse for you."

I practically ran to the nurse's station and begged her to come right away. She immediately went to Will's side but told me to wait outside the ward while she examined him. When she came out of the ward, she stopped me from going back in. "He's very weak and needs his rest. Visiting is over for him today."

"I understand," I said quietly as my spirits nosedived. "May I please at least say goodbye? I'll make it quick."

The nurse relented and I went back into his ward. His eyes were closed again, but I sensed he was still awake. I leaned over him and whispered in his ear. "The nurse says I have to go now so you can rest, but I'll be back tomorrow. I'm here for you, Will, and I always will be. Because I love you."

His eyes slowly opened, beholding mine in earnest. I kissed his lips. "Bye, my love. See you tomorrow."

I left the hospital so deep in worry over his condition that I prayed all the way home.

*   *   *

Late May

Daniel took me to see Will every day. Each day, his pain lessened as his condition slowly improved but I never got the chance to be alone with him again. The morning was a busy time for him with the medical staff who attended to him so I came later in the day. Madeline arrived every day around lunchtime and spent the afternoon with him along with a steady stream of Will's many friends and business associates who dropped in to see him.

One morning, I had gone out to the back terrace for some fresh air when I saw Adrienne walking toward her cottage. No doubt she'd been up to the guard shack for her morning visit with Chet. She wore a beautiful dress today in royal blue. I waved. Instead of going into her cottage, she turned and walked toward the terrace. I ran down the steps and met her halfway across the yard.

"Hello," Adrienne said as we approached each other. I asked her to join me on the terrace to get out of the hot sun and cool down with some iced tea. She accepted and we began to walk toward the house. "Have you been to the hospital to see Will today?"

184

"No." I shielded my eyes from the bright sun with my hand. "Daniel and I usually slip out for an hour or two in the afternoon, but he had pressing business to attend to this afternoon."

Adrienne squinted. "Will you make it today? Errol is going to the nursery this afternoon to pick up his order of summer flowers to plant along the driveway."

I found her knowledge of Errol's schedule to be rather interesting. She seemed to know the movements of the men on my payroll better than I did. "Oh, that's right," I said, disappointed that I'd forgotten all about Errol needing to go on an errand. I'd have to wait until he returned.

Unless I drove myself...

"How long is Will expected to be in the hospital?" Adrienne asked as we slowly walked up the stone steps.

"I don't know, but I don't think he'll be ready to go home any time soon."

Adrienne stopped for a moment. "If you'd like some company, I'd love to go with you and Daniel one of these days."

The idea delighted me. "How about today? I'll drive us there."

Adrienne's wide smile indicated she found my offer irresistible. "I'd love that. Shall we go before dinner or afterward?"

I thought about that as we resumed climbing the steps. "Why don't we stop somewhere for dinner first then go to the hospital? Visiting hours are until eight o'clock."

"C'est magnifique!" Adrienne stopped again. "If you don't mind, I'd like to go back to the cottage instead of having tea. I need to decide on what to wear and get ready."

She needed several hours to get ready? The old Adrienne was back!

"Of course," I said. "I have some things to take care of as well. I'll

185

pick you up at four o'clock. Okay?"

She was already hurrying back down the steps. She confirmed her agreement to the meeting time with a wave of her hand. I needed to tell Cook that I was skipping dinner and make her promise to keep my evening plans quiet. I felt guilty about excluding Francie, but I wanted to get to know Adrienne better and this outing would be a step in the right direction.

Gerard greeted me in the hall. "You have a visitor, My Lady. He insisted on waiting for you in the den."

Harv was the only person I knew who would wait in there—where I kept a locked safe filled with expensive liquor. By the time I arrived, he'd already opened the safe and pulled out a case to take home.

I stood at the door and watched him close the safe. When he turned, he smiled but the hard lines on his face told me something in him had changed. I instinctively knew what it was and that things would never be the same between us again. "So, you're back from Chicago," I said evenly and shut the door. "I gather you're here in response to the message I left with Marv."

"Sit down, honey." He pulled out my desk chair. "We need to talk."

Chapter Seventeen

To my surprise and delight, Daniel arrived home in time to accompany Adrienne and me for the evening. He started my car and I drove it along the back driveway to the door of the cottage, hoping Adrienne wouldn't take her time because I didn't want to risk Francie seeing me through one of the back windows of the house. Adrienne came out almost immediately, wearing a gold and burgundy dress and carrying a matching shawl. Daniel assisted her into the car, got in next to her, and slammed the door shut.

I sped down the driveway, hoping Francie was on the telephone with her best friend and hadn't heard all the noise. As I drove through the gates we waved to Hal. He'd just come on duty. I turned onto Summit Avenue.

The wind blew my hair, messing up my carefully arranged pin curls, but I didn't care. This was the first time I'd driven my car since the night I bought groceries for my dinner with Will and it felt good to be motoring along without a care in the world.

We stopped at a small café that Daniel suggested and the three of us spent a leisurely two hours chatting over dinner. I insisted on picking up the tab.

When we got back on the road and stopped at our first stoplight,

Adrienne smiled wistfully. "I envy you for taking it upon yourself to learn how to drive. It must give you so much freedom."

"I'm so glad I did. Will taught me," I said. "It took a little while to catch on, but it wasn't difficult. I simply needed to practice."

"Would you like to learn?" Daniel asked Adrienne as he rested his arm across the back of the seat. "I'll teach you."

She gasped with excitement. "Oh, yes! I'd love to learn how to drive. Someday when I'm performing again, I'm going to save for a car." She splayed her hand on the dashboard. "If I had transportation, I wouldn't have to depend on anyone else. I could take care of myself."

"I'll make sure you get a super deal if you want a Ford," I said with a laugh, knowing firsthand how she felt about being free. I wanted to simply give her a car, but I knew she was too proud to accept such an extravagant gift from me.

I found a parking spot on the backside of the hospital building. The sunny day had turned cloudy, but it didn't feel like rain yet.

When we entered Will's ward, we found him sitting in a wheelchair. He seemed genuinely surprised to see us. I was surprised but thrilled that we were his only visitors.

"Hello, Will," I said in my sweetest voice. "I'm happy to see you're doing so well today."

He grinned as he sat back in his chair. He wore a beige robe over his green hospital gown. "I'll be doing a *lot* better once I spring from this joint and get back to work. The first thing I'm going to do when I get out of here is to buy myself a nice steak dinner."

The steak dinner remark made me smile. To me, his growing appetite proved he was definitely on the mend. I stood next to him, wishing he and I were alone. "Speaking of food, I brought you something." I held up a cloth bag. "Cook baked you some cookies and she got a little carried away, but I'm sure you won't mind."

His gaze shot to the bag. "Really?"

I could tell by the surprise in his voice he was desperate for anything other than hospital food. He reached for the bag and tore open the waxed paper. He pulled out a man-sized cookie and devoured half of the large, soft treat in one bite. "Hmmm...oatmeal-raisin, my favorite," he said, his mouth stuffed with cookie pieces.

"There are eleven more in the bag. She gave you a dozen molasses cookies, too."

He glanced around. Most of his ward mates were busy with medical personnel or visitors. "Do you mind if I share these later with the guys?" When I replied it was fine with me, he grinned. "Next time you see Cook, give her a big kiss for me."

I had a better idea. I wanted him to kiss *me* first so I could pass it on but given the fact that he was no longer officially my beau or my bodyguard, I wasn't sure how to proceed with *that* request.

Will offered each of us a cookie and then stuffed the bag under the pillow on his bed. "Ladies," he said with amusement as he handed each of us a Pep-O-Mint candy, "would you like to step outside for a while? I could use some fresh air."

The four of us left the ward together. Daniel pushed Will's wheelchair, steering him toward the front entrance. Once we were outside, Daniel parked Will's chair near a visitor's bench. The wind had picked up, becoming blustery at times.

"Adrienne," Daniel said happily, "why don't we take a walk around the grounds and give these kids some privacy?"

I almost laughed at his veiled attempt to get Adrienne all to himself, but I kept a straight face and waved as they left us. I couldn't wait to be alone with Will.

Will reached over and patted the wooden bench. "Come here."

I sat down and wasted no time getting right to the point. "Will, about the night of the ambush—"

"I meant what I said."

I stared at him, amazed. "You remember lying on the sidewalk and whispering in my ear?"

He turned his chair toward me and took my hands in his. "Hey…it's not every day a guy is stretched out on the ground bleeding his guts out and seeing his entire life pass before his eyes. I kept seeing your face and it made me realize what a fool I'd been." His eyes studied mine. "I remember every word. I said, 'If I don't make it, I love you.' I knew it might be my only chance to tell you what I'd been lying to myself about all along—that I was better off without you." The longing in his deep blue eyes left no doubt he was telling the truth. "Ever since that day, I've wanted to take you in my arms and tell you again, but with me flat on my back and so many people around all the time, it was impossible to get some time alone with you. Char…"

Gingerly, he rose from the chair. I scooted over, allowing him to sit next to me on the bench. I didn't care if the entire world saw us. I leaned close and slid my arms around his neck. His long arms gently circled me as his lips claimed mine. My stomach danced with giddiness. I should have been laughing with relief, but strangely, tears stung my eyes. I wanted this so much, but part of me was afraid to believe him. Was it really true? Would this moment open the door to a lifetime together or would he change his mind later? "I love you, so much," I whispered breathlessly in his ear, "but I've never been shy about expressing my feelings."

Cupping my face in his hands, he tilted my head back and kissed me again. "After that night we spent together, I knew without a doubt you were the one for me. When I came to see you the next day, I almost asked you to marry me. I knew I was way in over my head with you, but I wanted to make things right. I stopped short of posing the question because I realized it was too soon to press you."

Oh, my gosh.

"Oh, Will, I wish you would have asked because I'd have said yes in a heartbeat!" A proposal would have had my heart flipping cartwheels!

He let out a long sigh as he brushed a tear from the corner of my eye with his thumb. "Then I found out you'd become entangled with Harv Katzenbaum and everything fell apart."

"About Harv—"

"Let's not talk about that now. I don't want anything to interrupt this moment." Slowly, he eased himself off the bench to a standing position. I stood up and pressed my cheek against his chest. He wrapped his arms around me again and kissed me, but his labored breathing warned me his wound was causing him pain.

I tried to pull away. "Will, you need to sit down."

"No, stay here," he said and kissed me again. "Just let me hold you."

We stood quietly in each other's arms for a while then I gently eased away from him. I needed him to hear this…

"Harv and I had a serious talk this morning. We agreed it wasn't in our best interests to associate with each other for a while. Maybe for good."

"What?" He stared at me, stunned. "What happened?"

"Harv has changed. I barely know him anymore." I stepped back and gazed across the grounds. "He met with some very powerful people in Chicago to set up new distribution channels for his business and returned with a group of mercenaries on his payroll." I looked up. "Anyway, he came to see me today because I told him I refused to be shackled to his bodyguards any longer. He told me that if I won't accept his protection, I'm a liability to him. So, for now, we're going our separate ways."

"You did the right thing." Will placed his hands on my shoulders. "I know how much he means to you, but in time, you'll see it's for the best."

"The next step is to sell off everything," I said seriously. "If I have to choose between the life I inherited and you, Will, I choose *you*."

His eyes softened. "You don't need to do that."

"Why not? Isn't that what you wanted?"

He shook his head. "Not anymore." The breeze blew a lock of wavy black hair across his forehead. Reaching up slowly, he slipped his fingers through it, combing it back. "I was wrong to expect you to turn your life completely upside down for me."

"You already did that when you said it was over between us then came back as my bodyguard," I said, sticking out my lower lip. "You were so bossy and cross. I'm glad that's over."

He lifted one brow. "So, you're trying to fire me again, are you?"

Curling my fingers around the lapels of his robe, I raised on my tiptoes and kissed him. "I like to think of it as giving you a promotion."

He let out a wry chuckle. "Promoted to what? Did Gerard quit?"

Laughing, I playfully pretended to sock his jaw. "You're my main man now."

"You'd better mean I'm your *only* man," he replied gruffly. "If I knew I could keep you under lock and key until I got out of this place, I'd marry you in a minute."

I squealed. "So, let's get married! Right now! Adrienne and Daniel will be our witnesses."

His smile faded as the tip of his finger burned a tingling trail down the side of my neck. Desire smoldered in his eyes. "Baby, there's *no way*

I'm spending my wedding night in this hospital. There isn't going to be any marriage until I'm back in perfect shape."

My heart soared. "Are you proposing to me?"

He lifted my chin with his thumb. His eyes pierced mine. "Not until I can get down on one knee and do it right."

"I'll wait!" I laughed, my eyes spilling over with tears of joy. "For as long as it takes."

* * *

It was nearly dark by the time we left the hospital. I kissed Will goodbye, wishing I could stay longer, but his eyelids were starting to droop with fatigue. The wind raged through the swirling treetops, ferociously whipping around us as we walked out of the hospital. Adrienne and I clutched at our skirts to keep them from flapping in our faces.

We walked along the side of the building past the few vehicles still parked in that area. Once we came upon my Ford, Adrienne and I stood off to one side, happily waiting for Daniel to start the car. He walked to the driver's side and opened the door to adjust the controls. The moment he stepped behind the door a dark figure appeared. I didn't have time to warn him before he turned his head toward the sound of crunching gravel. The figure suddenly raised his arm and swiftly came down, smashing Daniel on the side of the head. Adrienne and I screamed as Daniel collapsed on the ground and Ralph Dixon emerged with a pistol in his hand.

Adrienne gasped and clutched at her heart. "Ralph! What have you done?"

"Shut up!" he ordered and waved the pistol toward a nearby wooded area. "Move!"

We obeyed, walking deeper and deeper into the inky darkness as we trudged away from the hospital and toward the dense underbrush in the woods. I could barely see Adrienne's face, but that didn't stop me from sensing her heart-stopping fear. She knew a lot more about this man than I did, and her terror of him surrounded both of us like an ominous aura.

She stumbled over something on the ground. Reaching out, I grabbed her arm to keep her from falling. Her mesh handbag accidentally swung against me. Something hard inside it hit the back of my hand.

Ralph slammed his hand against her back, nearly knocking her off her feet. "I said, keep moving!"

His cruelty toward her angered me. "Where are you taking us?" I demanded.

Ralph snatched me by the arm and swung me around. "What did you say?"

My eyes had become accustomed to the dark and his face was so close to mine I nearly fainted. "I—I want to know where you're taking us," I repeated timidly. "What do you want?"

"I want Gus to *spin in his grave*." The howling wind made his voice sound like a raspy stage whisper. "He deserves to lose everything. Like I did!"

My heart jumped to my throat. "But…w-why hurt us? What did we ever do to you?"

"Gus' whores—both of you!" He shoved me to the ground and cocked his pistol close to my face. "Wiggling your little fanny on the dance floor of my club. Gettin' the boys so worked up they ripped the place apart over you!"

"That wasn't my fault! Leonard Murtagh started the fight."

"He deserves to rot in prison!" Ralph spat in the dark. "Makes big promises but never delivers!"

I suddenly realized something; Ralph was the silent partner

Leonard bragged about when he wanted me to reopen La Coquette. When that fell through, he must have crowed to Ralph that he could get his hands on my money if Ralph would make me a partner in the Tansy Club. That obviously upset Ralph, causing him to order a murderous rampage the night he saw us at Tresanti's.

Ralph grabbed me by the neck and pulled me to my feet. "Shut up and get going!"

We began to march again. Adrienne's fear kept her silent, but her sniffling warned me she was crying. I knew once we entered the woods we were at the point of no return. My mind spun in panic. What were we going to do?

Adrienne swallowed a sob. I grabbed her hand and squeezed it, encouraging her to be strong. As long as I had a breath in me, I wasn't giving up. My son wasn't going to grow up an orphan. Not if I could help it.

At the edge of the woods, I stopped, refusing to go any farther.

Ralph shoved me so hard I nearly fell. Getting my bearings, I spun around and grabbed onto the hand that held his gun. I began to struggle with him, trying to get it away. I screamed to make as much noise as possible, hoping the wind carried it toward the houses on the other side of the field. Unfortunately, the wind was so fierce most of the residents probably had their windows closed. Even so, it was worth a try. "Holler for help, Adrienne!"

Something white flashed in the corner of my eye.

"Stop!" Adrienne held up a small pistol with both hands, her handbag dangling from her wrist. Even in the dark, I could see her arms shaking uncontrollably. "Or I'll—I'll shoot!"

In one swift move, Ralph Dixon let go of me and backhanded Adrienne, knocking her to the ground. "You stupid whore! I should have killed you when Gus was alive. To watch him grieve!"

The gun had flown from her hand, landing on the ground between us. It was a small-caliber handgun with a mother-of-pearl handle—exactly like the one Gus had given me. Even in the hysteria of the moment, I knew that was no coincidence. Gus had armed both of us for a reason and now I realized why. His words ricocheted through my mind—

If you're going to point a weapon at someone, you'd better be ready to use it.

Ralph raised his arm to slam Adrienne in the face. In a split-second decision, I snatched her gun from the ground.

If you've only got one shot, you'd better make it count.

I pointed the gun at Ralph and pulled the trigger. The bullet hit him in the thigh.

Oh, dear, God!

I'd made a fatal mistake and thought he would kill me now, but I didn't count on the pain distracting him. Spewing profanity, he reached down to clutch the wound and I stepped closer, gripping the gun with both hands. I pulled the trigger again, hoping the chamber held more than one bullet.

The shot slammed into his chest.

I held my breath as Ralph Dixon went silent and crumpled to the ground. I stared at his lifeless body, not knowing if I'd killed him or merely wounded him, but I wasn't sticking around to find out. I shoved Adrienne's gun into my pocket then found Ralph's gun where it dropped from his hand and kicked it into the underbrush. If he did regain consciousness, he wouldn't find it.

"Adrienne," I said hurriedly as I ran to where she lay on the ground next to Ralph, sobbing uncontrollably. "Come on. We have to get out of here. Now!" I tried to get her up, but she wouldn't move. I was so keyed up that I grabbed her by the arm and pulled on it as hard as I could. I got her to sit up and then helped her to her feet. I managed to grip my arm around her waist and together, we stumbled our way across the field to get back to the car.

When we got there, Daniel was gone. A spot of blood remained on the ground where he'd lain.

"Where's Daniel?" Adrienne cried. "I've got to find Daniel!"

"Someone must have found him and brought him into the hospital," I said as I pulled her around to the passenger side. "Let's get the car started first then we'll drive around and see if we can find him."

"*Oh, mon Dieu.* Where's my purse?" she cried. "I've lost my purse!"

"I'll get it, Adrienne. Please, just get into the car."

She must have dropped it when Ralph knocked her to the ground. I cringed at the thought of having to go back there again, but we couldn't leave it behind. I helped her into the passenger side and ran back to the area, shivering at the eerie silhouette of Ralph's motionless body. *Hurry up*, I told myself, gasping for breath as I frantically looked around. I finally found her purse and bolted back to the car as fast as I could. By the time I reached the Ford, my knees wobbled fiercely.

With shaking hands, I managed to start the car and drove around to the entrance, stopping next to another parked vehicle. Under the exterior light, I saw Daniel sitting hunched over on a bench, holding a bloody hand to the side of his head. He hung his head low, appearing to be dazed or in extreme pain.

"There he is!" Adrienne cried.

"He needs medical attention. Stay here. I'll go and help him walk into the hospital."

I left the car running and ran to assist him. "Daniel! Wait here and I'll get help."

He reached out and clutched my arm. "I don't know what happened. I don't remember anything!"

"It's okay, Daniel," I said as I leaned close and tried to examine the wound on the side of his head. "I need to get you into the hospital so the staff can take care of your injury."

"No!" Daniel forcefully pushed me away. "You're not dragging me in there. They'll take my clothes away and confine me to a bed. I need to find out who hit me!" He stood up and started to stumble away.

"But Daniel—"

"I said no!"

"Okay, I'll take you home," I replied desperately, realizing he wasn't thinking clearly, "but you need to get in the car. *Now.*"

Adrienne left the car and ran over to us, grabbing Daniel by the arm. "You're coming home with me, *ma Cherie*! I'll take care of you."

I took his other arm and helped him walk to the Ford. We got him inside and shut the door. Then Adrienne and I climbed in through the other side and I drove away. I needed to get them far, far away from here. No one must ever connect us to what happened in the field a block from this hospital.

Once we were on our way, Adrienne began to sob again. Sitting next to her, I glanced her way and nearly gasped at the condition of her face. Her eye had begun to swell. A large, dark spot covered her sharp cheekbone. "Ralph used to beat you, didn't he," I stated quietly. "He abused you when you were his girlfriend."

Adrienne nodded silently as she wiped her tears away with the back of her hands.

I gripped the steering wheel in anger. "He'll never hurt you again."

"Gus knew what Ralph was doing to me," she said tearfully. "He saw me one day trying to hide a bruise with makeup and he promised me that if I left Ralph, he'd always protect me. He gave me a job and an apartment." Her voice cracked. "I owe my life to Gus."

My heart throbbed with guilt at the times I'd railed at Gus about her. If I'd only known... Still, I didn't excuse Gus for having an affair with her. In his own way, he'd tried to be good to Adrienne by protecting her, but in making her his mistress, he'd taken advantage of her, too. And been unfaithful to me.

"The night of the ambush, Francie heard the cops say the attack was to get revenge on Gus," I said as the answer became clear in my mind. "At the time, I didn't understand what they meant, but now I realize Ralph was behind it. He was trying to punish everyone in connection with Gus."

Adrienne turned her head. Fresh tears streamed down her swollen face. "If you hadn't taken me in and given me the cottage, I would have been forced to go back to him. I don't know how I'll ever repay you."

"You already did," I said seriously and patted my pocket. "You supplied the gun that got us out of that jam. That's all the repayment I need."

Adrienne managed a sad, but grateful smile.

Chapter Eighteen

As soon as I arrived home and helped Adrienne assist Daniel into her cottage, I parked the car in front of the garage, took the back way into the house via the terrace, and ran upstairs to my room. I didn't want anyone to see the grass and bloodstains on my dress, not to mention the smell of gunpowder. I tore the dress off and hid it in Gus' secret room along with Adrienne's gun. When Lillian asked about my dress, I planned to tell her I'd given it to Adrienne. Never mind that it was too small for her. Lillian might think it odd but wouldn't question it.

I filled the bathtub with hot water and soaked my weary body, trying to wash away all traces of what happened tonight.

The next morning, I went to the cottage to see how Adrienne and Daniel were faring. Daniel was doing better, but I was dismayed to see what Ralph had done to Adrienne. One eye was nearly swollen shut and the dark bruise on her cheekbone had spread across one side of her face. She stared at the floor as she let me in, visibly ashamed of her appearance. It angered me deeply to see how *one man* had deliberately destroyed not only her appearance but her fragile self-esteem. I thought about the women and girls taking refuge at Anna's House and I was determined to help as many as I could.

I hugged her and insisted she let me know if she needed *anything*.

All she asked for was a new shirt for Daniel.

Adrienne had cleaned up Daniel's wound and discarded his bloody shirt. He sat up in bed drinking coffee when I went into the bedroom to check on him. The grave look in his eyes told me she had filled him in on everything. "You're a mighty strong woman, Char."

"I did what I had to do," I said soberly as I sat on the edge of the bed. "If he'd gone after me alone, I don't know if I'd have been able to save myself, but seeing him take out his hatred on Adrienne gave me an inner strength I didn't know I had. When Ralph knocked the gun from her hand, I just acted on instinct." I exhaled a shaky breath. "It feels like a bad dream."

"You need permanent bodyguards," he argued. "As soon as possible."

I nodded. "I plan to hire some immediately."

Daniel considered that as he sipped his coffee. "If I know Will, he'll expect to take on that task himself." Daniel's gaze met Adrienne's. "Both of us will."

After I left Adrienne's cottage, I found the car where I had parked it the night before and was glad Errol hadn't had time yet to move it into the garage. I started it and drove to the hospital, hoping to get a few minutes alone with Will again.

When I arrived, my heart fluttered with trepidation. The field was crawling with coppers. A dozen or so vehicles were parked around the crime scene, blocking it from the public. Staring straight ahead, I swallowed hard and walked toward the hospital entrance. I passed by the spot where I'd parked last night and checked the gravel for Daniel's blood. Luckily, we'd had a heavy downpour in the middle of the night and all visible traces of the blood had been washed away.

When I arrived at Will's ward, I found his bed empty—stripped bare. A new patient lay sleeping in the bed next to his. What had happened to Will?

I turned around and ran to the nurse's station. "Where is Will Van Elsberg?" I asked the nurse on duty.

"He checked himself out this morning," the young nurse replied. "Doctor Hedin examined him around eleven o'clock. Then he left."

I stared at her in amazement. Will hadn't mentioned yesterday the possibility of checking out. I thanked her and went home, wondering if he'd stopped there first. According to my staff, he hadn't been there. I called his house, but the telephone simply rang and rang.

By late afternoon, I'd paced the floor until I couldn't stand it. Bringing a casserole with me that Cook had prepared especially for Will, I started my car and drove to his house on Laurel Avenue. If he wasn't there, I planned to wait in the house until he came home.

I nearly swallowed my tongue in surprise when I turned off Dale Street onto Laurel Avenue. Cars lined both sides of the street so far down the block I had to park at the entrance to Holcomb Circle. Echoing through the open windows of his house, jazz music coming from his Victrola traveled all the way to my car.

I grabbed the casserole dish from the front seat and walked to the house. Gingerly, I crossed his front sidewalk, bolted up the stairs, and crossed the wraparound porch to the front door. The house was jammed with people and the cacophony of their chatter and laughter competed with the music.

A young woman saw me peering through the screen door into the foyer. "Hi!" she said in a perky, bird-like voice as she opened the door to welcome me. "Come on in and join the party!" She saw the casserole dish in my hands. "If that's for the buffet, just put it in the kitchen." She giggled. "If you can find an open spot on the counter."

If I can squeeze between all of these people, you mean...

I got as far as the dining room before the log jam of bodies stopped me completely. Frustrated, I looked around to see if I could find either Will or Madeline.

Someone in the crowd squeezed by me, causing the people on my right to move. Looking between them, I peered into the living room and saw Will sitting on the sofa between two pretty blondes. His face was pale and he looked tired, but most of all, he looked bored. That surprised me. He used to have parties every weekend when I worked as his housekeeper. I spent every Friday cooking and cleaning to get ready for them.

Just the same, I was upset—and hurt—he hadn't called me to let me know he was home.

Deciding to leave, I jostled my way through the crowd and placed the casserole in the kitchen then I maneuvered my way back to the front door and walked out. I crossed the porch but paused at the top of the steps when I heard the spring stretching on the screen door.

"Where are you going?"

I slowly turned around at the sound of his voice. The first time we met, we were standing exactly in the same places we were now. Oh, how much things between us had changed since then! "I'm going home."

"Why?" He let the screen door slam behind him as he slowly walked toward me, leaning heavily on his cane. "You just got here."

I glared at him. "I wasn't invited."

He shrugged. "Neither was I. The gang was already in the house when we got home. Maddie's friends—they started the party without us." His jaw tightened. "I guess this has been going on every night since I was hospitalized, but I told my sister it ends *today*. My house isn't the neighborhood speakeasy."

He looked so exhausted I doubted he had the strength to keep going much less clear the place out. It worried me. He needed peace and quiet. A comfortable place to rest. "Why didn't you tell me you were leaving the hospital this morning?"

"I didn't know it myself until the doctor examined me. He said I was recovering well and that's when I decided I could heal the rest of the way at home." He gripped one hand on the newel post for support. "When Maddie showed up, I told her to get me some clothes because I was checking myself out."

"I was worried about you," I said, playing with a button on the open collar of his white shirt. "I didn't know where you'd gone and no one answered the telephone at your house when I called."

"Maddie drove straight from the hospital to a restaurant to buy me that steak I've been talking about. I just wanted to go home, but she insisted so I let her take me out to lunch." He reached out. "Come here."

I moved close and nestled my cheek on his chest.

"The entire time I was stuck in that hospital bed, I couldn't get you out of my mind," he murmured as he rested his chin on the top of my head. "I've been a fool to think I could get along without you." He kissed the top of my head. "Look at me."

I looked up. His deep blue eyes were etched with fatigue but not too tired to communicate how much he desired me. "I love you, Char. More than you will ever know."

"Oh, Will, I—" My reply was silenced by his kiss.

"Hey, has anybody seen Will?" The voice sounded like Madeline's.

"Yeah! He's out on the porch lockin' lips with some gorgeous dame," a masculine voice gleefully shouted.

A scratching sound signaled someone had jerked the tonearm off the record playing on the Victrola. The house went quiet except for the thundering of feet as a herd of people crowded in front of the parlor windows.

"Let's get out of here," Will whispered.

"I know just the place. It's as quiet as a tomb and my staff will relish fussing over you."

With arms locked around each other's waist, we slowly descended the steps.

The screen door creaked open. "Will! Where are you going?"

Without turning back, Will waved. "Bye, Maddie."

"But, Will—"

He ignored her. "Did you drive yourself, Char, or is Errol waiting for you?"

I laughed. "I drove myself, of course."

Will stopped at the end of his stone walk. "When we get to your house, we're going to have a serious talk."

"Look, I know what you're going to say—"

"We're going to come to an understanding." His eyes narrowed. "And I don't want any backtalk out of you. Get that? If we're going to make this relationship work, you *will* listen to me—or else."

"Or else—what?" I retorted, pouting. I figured he'd heard about Ralph Dixon at the hospital, and though he hadn't said anything yet, he would grill me once we got home. And I would confess my part in it. It wouldn't do any good to deny it. He'd simply get the full story from Daniel.

He sighed. "Char, Char…what am I going to do with you?"

I smiled mischievously and gripped his shirt collar. "What do you want to do with me?"

"Take you over my knee," he grumbled, "then kiss you senseless and show you how much I love you."

"Two out of three isn't bad," I said coyly. "I'll take the last two."

"Don't tempt me, you little fox." He grinned. "Baby, when I get this body back in shape…"

I glowed inside with happiness. The old Will was back and that was all that mattered.

The End, but…

The story of Char and Will continues in…

The Bootlegger's Legacy

Book Three of the Moonshine Madness Series

It's June 1926 in St. Paul, Minnesota, and Charlotte LeDoux is determined to reinvent herself.

Her late husband, a notorious bootlegger, left her a Summit Avenue mansion, a secret room filled with cash, and a reputation riddled with bullet holes. Char is desperate to rebuild her identity as an honest entrepreneur, but her plans falter when she repeatedly encounters unfair bias. Then she learns that one foolish mistake with her beau has left her in the family way— the final blow to not only her character but her aspirations as well. She realizes it's time to marry the man she loves and turn her life in a new direction. That is, until she learns he has betrayed her trust. Her belief in Will and in true love is shattered.

Will Van Elsberg is a tough private investigator, but he's no match for his headstrong gal. He's so madly in love with Char, however, that he'll do whatever it takes to keep her safe. When he learns she's pregnant, he's anxious to tie the knot. Instead, their engagement is doomed after Char discovers he's withheld crucial information from her. He's determined to tell her everything to win back her trust, but the situation changes when Char suddenly goes missing and he finds a ransom note in her car. Facing an unknown enemy who holds all the cards, Will is thrust into the greatest crisis of his life—to rescue a woman carrying his child who means more to him than life itself.

Get your copy today!

Minnie's Homemade Wine Recipes

(Based on actual handwritten recipes from the past!)

Fruit Wine

Put clean, washed fruit (blackberries, elderberries, raspberries, culled strawberries or wild grapes) into a stoneware crock, mashing down a shallow layer, adding more fruit, mashing that, etc. until all fruit is used.

Pour lukewarm water almost to the top. Cover with cheesecloth to eliminate the problem with flies and allow to stand in a warm spot until it is fermenting well.

When it is bubbling good and has a "yeasty" smell, strain off the juice and measure. In a gallon jug, place the juice to a depth of about ¼ to ⅓ the capacity of the jug; add sugar water to fill.

The raw sugar syrup mixture should be made with 5 cups of sugar diluted in enough water to fill the rest of the jar.

Cover the mouth of the jug with cheesecloth to allow air in and keep flies out.

Let stand in a warm spot for several months to ferment.

When liquid no longer bubbles, but is clear and quiet, strain and store in fruit jars in a cool place to age.

Wines may be tried at Christmastime but improve with age.

Elderberry Wine

Cook 9 pounds of sugar in 3 gallons of water for a half-hour then drop 2 quarts of ripe elderberries into the syrup and let stand until cool. Add 1½ cakes of compressed yeast and let stand one week, stirring daily.

Then add 1 pound of seedless raisins. Let stand 3 months in a stone crock or jar.

Strain and bottle.

If not sweet enough, add sugar to taste.

Two lemons and three oranges can be used with the berries if you wish instead of the raisins.

Dandelion Wine

1 full quart blossoms

1 gallon of water

1 lemon, cut into slices (not peeled)

2½ pounds of sugar

Put all together in a kettle and boil for 5 minutes then pour into a jar.

When cool, add two tablespoons of yeast. Keep in a warm place for three days until it ferments and stops working.

Then strain and bottle, not cork, tightly.

Rhubarb Wine

5 pounds of rhubarb

1 gallon of water

Let stand one week; stir every day. Then strain through a cloth and add 3½ pounds of sugar and the juice of 2 lemons. Put in a jar to ferment. Add 1 small package of yeast. When done, bottle.

Want to find more authors who write sweet romance?

Join my reader group - Happily Ever After Stories. If you like sweet romance and want to be part of a great group that has lots of fun and fantastic parties, visit us at:

https://www.facebook.com/groups/HEAstories/.

More books by Denise Devine

Christmas Stories

Merry Christmas, Darling

A Christmas to Remember

A Merry Little Christmas

Once Upon a Christmas

Mistletoe and Wine – ***Coming Soon!***

A Very Merry Christmas - Hawaiian Holiday Series

~*~

Bride Books

The Encore Bride

Lisa – Beach Brides Series

Ava – Perfect Match Series

Della – ***Coming Soon!***

~*~

Moonshine Madness Series – Historical Suspense/Romance

The Bootlegger's Wife – Book 1

Guarding the Bootlegger's Widow – Book 2

The Bootlegger's Legacy – Book 3

The Nightingale Detective Agency – Book 4 – ***Coming Soon!***

~*~

West Loon Bay Series – Small Town Romance

Small Town Girl – Book 1

Brown-Eyed Girl – Book 2

Country Girl – Book 3 - ***Coming Soon!***

Cozy Mystery
Unfinished Business

Dark Fortune

Girl Friday Cozy Series
Shot in the Dark – Book 1

The Accidental Detective – *Coming Soon!*

~*~

This Time Forever - an inspirational romance

Romance and Mystery Under the Northern Lights – short stories

~*~

Want more? Read the first chapter of Denise's most popular novels on her blog at:
https://deniseannette.blogspot.com

Audio Books Galore!
Do you like audiobooks?

Many of the above books are available in audio!

Check out Denise's website for links to each audiobook.

https:www.deniseannettedevine.com

Narrated by Lorana L. Hoopes

Monthly sales!

Made in the USA
Las Vegas, NV
31 July 2023

75488086R00118